unravel

unravel

Preeti Singh

First published in India in 2014 by:

Preeti Singh

preetisinghbooks@gmail.com

Copyright © 2014 Preeti Singh

Print Book ISBN: 9789384439187

Preeti Singh asserts the moral right to be identified as the author of this work.

Cover design by Maritza Gonzalez

Publishing facilitation: AuthorsUpFront

Also available as an eBook on Amazon Kindle, Apple iTunes, Google Play, Kobo and Nook.

may you find yourself here

unravel

Earliest known use of word – 1603
un·rav·el verb \ n- ra-v l\

: to cause the separate threads of something to come
  apart
: to find the correct explanation for something that is
  difficult to understand
: to fail or begin to fail

Contents

Veera

This is not the way I thought I would go, laid up on a cold white bed at the Lilavati Hospital. In a coma, as I hear them say.

Whenever I thought of death, I would picture myself lying in my bed at home, with my children and grandchildren around me. In the final chapter of my life, I am surrounded by my family and friends who love me. I have a little speech for each of them—a little nugget of wisdom that they will cherish for the rest of their lives. I hold my children's hands and gently breathe my last. My son is stoic and my daughters inconsolable!

The influence of Hindi movies, I guess....

But I am not done yet! I am only 75. An active, independent 75-year-old. There is so much to be done, so many loose ends to tie, things to tell my children, pardons I must ask for. I want to see my grandchildren grow up. There is a marriage I pray for every day. And I still have to visit places on the map that my grandson Ranvir has put up on one of my bedroom walls. We mark each place I have visited with a red *bindi*, but there are many empty spots yet.

But then again, a split second is all it takes to change life. Why in God's name did I have to fall in the bathroom at an ungodly hour, when there was no one around to pick me up? Clearly, I don't choose my moments carefully.

I hear my children say that I am in one of the suites on the top floor of the Lilavati. I know the room from a previous visit. When I had come to meet little Meera, who lost her life at such a young age. It is the worst punishment God can give you—to snatch your child away from you while you look on helplessly.

I have an idea what the room looks like. You enter the living room area, which has sofas and a TV. The bedroom is beyond that and looks right into the Arabian Sea. It is a plush room, fitted with the best money can buy in Mumbai. KD would have insisted on putting me here. My son spares no expenses when it comes to me.

I remember remarking once that this floor of the Lilavati is so luxurious that you feel you have entered the lobby of a five-star hotel. Though of course, nothing eases the suffering or the pain. I feel no pain, but I can never forget Meera's pain or the haunted look on Nikki's face.

I can't open my eyes. I can't move my hands. I can't move any part of my body. I try to muster up the strength to show them I can hear them. That I understand what they are saying. To tell them I am alive. But my energy fails me. It's almost as if my body has become disconnected from me and refuses to obey my commands anymore.

I can hear my children in the room. Piya, my daughter, her husband, Anand, my son, KD, and my daughter-in-law, Mana. KD owns shares in one of the largest pharma companies in India, and sometime back, started dabbling in real estate too. When he finished his engineering and MBA, KD told me he was joining a big company that sells shampoo, soap, detergents and sanitary towels. I was horrified. He studied that hard to sell these things? I scraped and saved money to send him to Harvard so he could sell sanitary towels? Should men even be looking at such private feminine things and discussing what towels are good, and how many should sell in a month? I was so embarrassed. Should KD not have been in a bank, dealing with lots of money? What was the point of his studying to become an engineer? I thought I had made a mistake in not guiding him. Perhaps he would have been better off becoming a doctor. But then again, maybe I don't understand how the world works anymore.

The view from the big French windows in my room must be magnificent. You get a bird's-eye view of Bandra, BKC and the sea link that we Mumbaikars are so proud of. After 10 years and lots of money, when the sea link opened in 2009, connecting the western suburbs to Worli, it became a tourist hot spot. Everyone wanted to get on it and get a glimpse of Mumbai from a different angle. KD and his children went too. The traffic jam on the sea link got so bad that they left the driver to make his way out of it and walked back home! KD was irritated and railed against the incompetent traffic police, but the kids were so excited. On their way back, they stopped at Candies with him and ate all the goodies that Mana would not have allowed them to have. They brought back chicken sandwiches from there that both Mana and I enjoyed.

KD and Piya take turns keeping vigil in my room at night. I am not sure if I remain conscious throughout the day, or if these streams of consciousness are disjointed. I have no clue how many days I have been here, and whether it is day or night.

I figure it is morning if Piya is in the room and she comments, 'Mom, I got your favorite *poha* today. With loads of peanuts, just the way you like it.' Or 'Good thing, mom, you can't eat this. This tomato sandwich is full of butter.' KD is always on the phone. He works too hard. Sometimes I hear great agitation in his voice. He is telling someone to shut up. Or to stop threatening him. I hope my son is safe.

KD left selling shampoos and sanitary towels and started a factory to make medicines. Today he is worth more money than I had thought I would see in my lifetime, has employed more than a thousand people, and is a big man. I keep telling him that real estate is a dangerous business to be in, but my son refuses to listen to me. That kind of success begets enemies. I pray for his safety all the time.

I know when it is evening because it's time for visiting hours at the hospital. I recognize the voices of people who come in to visit me. They are all friends—mine, KD's, Piya's and Mana's. Mana and Anand's parents have also come to see me. They all talk as if I don't exist. Some of them talk in whispers, so I don't get disturbed. I feel like laughing out loud. Isn't it ironic? Something should disturb me so I can regain consciousness.

I wait for her, the one who refuses to visit me. And while I don't know the number of days I have been in this room, I know she has not come to visit me.

Sometimes I feel like there are cobwebs over my brain and my eyes. I imagine then that I am doing yoga and have assumed the *Shavasana* posture—lying on my back as if I were dead, with my hands on either side. Slowly, I tell myself to relax my toes, the heels, the soles of my feet. I travel up to my calves, willing them to get into a restful position, and then work up my body to my eyes. Patiently, I try to pry apart the web, one strand at a time, so that I may be able to look through the darkness and see some light.

When the cobwebs clear up, I see only two things—Namita, and my life in flashback.

I wish I could see Namita once more and hold her and kiss her. I struggle to come back from where I go. They say that when your life is about to end, you see all the events in your life with crystal clarity. I don't want to see those things.

I don't want to die—not yet.

Namita

To: namitap@gmail.com
From: Piyar@gmail.com
Jun 21, 2013
9 a.m.

Namita

Mom is in the hospital. She fell down in her bathroom sometime late last night. Mana found her there in the morning when she went to give Mom her tea. We brought her to Lilavati Hospital and she has been admitted here. She is in coma. The doctors think there is a burst aneurysm in her brain. They will be conducting more tests in the day.
Tried calling you but your number was unreachable. Call me ASAP.

To: namitap@gmail.com
From: Piyar@gmail.com
Jun 21, 2013
12.30 p.m.

Namita

Why haven't I heard from you? Can you at least call? KD and Mana have also been trying to get through to you. You may not like her, but she is your mother too Nams.

To: namitap@gmail.com
From: Piyar@gmail.com
Jun 21, 2013
5 p.m.

You are a strange one. Mom is in the hospital, and KD and I have been calling you incessantly. How can you hold on to your anger like this Namita? With your mother laid up in the hospital? You are abominable.
Call me. Write back. Asking anything more of you is too much I guess.

Ayesha

Ayesha stepped out of her bath and walked into the room wrapped in a towel. She glanced quickly at the time. There was still an hour to go before she met Shantanu. She had been on tenterhooks since last evening when he had called.

She had been out with Piya, helping her buy a dress for a party that weekend and was tired. Piya could take forever and Ayesha always wondered why she agreed to these shopping expeditions. Piya would go from one shop to another, trying dresses, examining herself from every possible angle. Putting her hair up, putting her hair down, wearing stilettos to check how the dress complemented her calves, walking around, sitting down...and then repeating the whole process with another dress. 'Phew, how much energy can you spend on one dress?' groaned Ayesha. It took her less than a minute to figure out if a shop had something that would appeal to her, another two minutes to try out the dress, and less than a minute to pay and exit the shop. All she could think of was coffee. And Ayesha promised herself that if Piya did not buy something in the next 10 minutes, they would head home. And she would not get emotionally blackmailed into a shopping expedition with Piya ever again.

So when her phone rang—it was an unknown number—Ayesha picked it up. She almost wished it was a call center executive on the other side, peddling a holiday, a low interest bank loan or a better mobile phone deal. She could then vent her irritation and rave and rant. When the voice on the other side asked if it was Ayesha, Ayesha heaved an impatient sigh and said, 'Speaking.'

There was a moment's pause and then the voice said, 'Hi. This is Shantanu. Remember me?'

Remember me? As if I ever forgot you, Ayesha wanted to say. But she was stunned, and muttered, 'How do you have my number?'

'We have common friends remember?'

Ayesha smiled, 'Of course we do. How are you? And whose number is this? Are you in Mumbai?'

'Steady, Chubby. One question at a time! Yes, I am in Mumbai for a day. On work. And I got your number from Ajay. I wanted to ask you if you would meet me.'

Ayesha went quiet. Shantanu hesitated on the phone. 'Look it's fine if you don't want to meet. I just thought we could.'

Fifteen years too late, thought Ayesha. *You called me 15 years too late.* How many times had she imagined picking up the phone and hearing Shantanu's voice? And how many times had she worked out in her mind, where and how they would meet again? Sometimes she thought she would meet him at the airport; he would be traveling alone, and so would she. And they both would change their seats to sit together and chat. Or perhaps their children would be at the same school and she would bump into him at a parent-teacher meeting.

Or at a restaurant in Pali Hill. Or at the gym. The possibilities were endless—in the line at the movies for popcorn, at the doctor's, at the traffic light, at a popular dining joint, in a bookshop. The phone call she had not thought of. The Shantanu she knew had kept his silence, the silence that was so deafening in the early years.

'Of course,' she said. 'We can meet. Till when are you here?'

—Till tomorrow evening.

—Hmm. Okay I can meet whenever you are free.

—Tomorrow evening then? I know you stay at Pali Hill. So, does Taj Lands End work for you?

—Sure. Will meet you in the lobby at six then.

Sucker, thought Ayesha. *I never did manage to play games with Shantanu. I was always available to him. When he wanted, I was at his beck and call. And I am doing the same thing again. Why did I not make him sweat? Tell him I would think about it and call him back? For 15 years, he has not contacted me and then he calls out of the blue. And the bugger knows I will meet him.*

Ayesha unwrapped the towel and gazed at her body in the full-length mirror. It was no longer the tight, young body that had melted under Shantanu's hands. In those days, Shantanu just had to look at her and she would melt. And when he touched her, every sound in the world was blocked out from her ears. Her blood roared into her ears and her heart would pound and she would feel hot, really hot. Now Ayesha saw the body of a mother—fuller breasts and hips, and marred by stretch marks. She traced her stretch marks and thought how she had hated them when the first ones had appeared.

They had marked her progress into motherhood. Today, she loved them—they reminded her of her children. Her body was not beautiful, not in the way a young girl's is, even though she worked out to keep herself in shape. And yet, she was most comfortable in her skin now! She wondered what Shantanu would think of her now. Fat, like all *Punju* women? Sexy still? Or would he not like what he saw?

Time had not really changed anything much, thought Ayesha as she rushed to avoid being late. She couldn't make up her mind about what to wear. Should she wear a regular T-shirt and jeans that made her look good, not hot or sexy? Or should she wear a dress? She definitely looked hotter in a dress. Or maybe a *kurti* over her jeans?

Eons ago, as a young girl who was giddy with excitement over meeting Shantanu, the process had been the same. She would agonize over what to wear, how to do her hair, what to accessorize her outfit with. Ayesha smiled to herself; *I bet Shantanu never noticed a single thing. He was too busy removing my clothes to notice what I wore anyway.*

Brushing her teeth, removing stray hairs from her chin, wearing her *kajal* and lipstick, spraying on some perfume…it felt the same—the wild thumping in her heart made Ayesha flush red at the thought of Shantanu.

When she was done, Ayesha critically examined herself in the mirror. And tried to drill sense into herself: 'You are no longer a young silly girl, Ayesha. And don't forget what he did to you.' For a moment, Ayesha felt defeated and wondered why she was going to meet him at all. She had told Piya about Shantanu's call and asked if she was doing the right thing by meeting him. And Piya had said, 'Life's too short, Ayesha. If you are curious about him and think you can handle meeting him again, go ahead. But will you tell Sid?'

Ayesha had totally forgotten about Sid! Her darling husband. Would she tell him? She had told Piya, 'I haven't thought about it. Do you think I should?'

'Do what your heart says, Ayesha. This is your decision.'

Ayesha could not get herself to tell Sid about meeting Shantanu that night. She had told Sid everything about Shantanu before they got married. Well, almost everything.

Maybe I will tell Sid later. I can tell him I just happened to bump into Shantanu.

Ayesha was terribly curious about meeting Shantanu. What had he turned into? How did he look? How was his marriage? His kids? And to see what she had lost.

Ayesha had been married for six months when she heard of Shantanu's marriage. She had broken down. There was a finality about his marriage. Like she would never get Shantanu again. Despite everything that had happened, Ayesha had hoped and prayed that Shantanu would realize he loved her and come back for her.

Even on her wedding day, Ayesha had prayed that Shantanu would walk in through the door—she would have walked out with him. Through the *mehndi*, through the *sangeet*, and even the actual wedding ceremony, she kept waiting for Shantanu. The guy she wanted to take *pheras* around the Guru Granth Sahib was Shantanu, not Sid.

On her honeymoon she thought of Shantanu. When she set up her home and brought her first fridge, she thought of Shantanu. When Sid made love to her, she thought of Shantanu. All that had mattered to her was Shantanu.

She had wept and wept on hearing about Shantanu's wedding and Piya had left work and spent the day with her—letting her talk, weep, agonize, and then weep some more.

Shantanu never came back for her after she left him. She remembered it as 'that heartbreak weekend'. And never forgot it, not once in the last 15 years. In the weeks leading up to that fateful weekend, Shantanu had become increasingly distant with her. Where he had once spoken of marriage and being with her, he had begun telling her he was not ready to commit right away. That he needed to settle down in his career. That his parents had other plans for him.

Dumb chick I was, Ayesha shook her head, as she drove to the Taj. She handed over her keys to the valet and smoothed down her dress. *Now I know better. If a guy wants you, nothing will keep him away from you. And if he wants you in his life, and wants to marry you, he will do just that. And if he doesn't, well, nothing you do will change his mind!*

Ayesha walked into the hotel, a bundle of nerves. Would she recognize him after so many years? She had tried looking for him on

Facebook but his profile picture had a guy in a black hood and cloak!

She looked around for him as her bags were being examined by the security lady and then she saw him...felt him, actually.

The tingle in her spine told her he was there. She felt his presence, like she always had. She turned and saw him walking towards her. He still had that swagger. And she looked up at his face. A large delighted smile lit up his face as he came close to her. He stopped a few steps away, put his hands in his pockets, and cocked his head. His eyes teased her, beckoned her, and as she walked those steps towards him, Shantanu's hands gathered her into an embrace. Ayesha let him hug her and breathed in deep. She was looking for a familiar fragrance. In the years gone by, she had agonized over how he smelt; she had been distraught when she realized one day that she had forgotten his smell. To her, forgetting that smell was losing him. Shantanu had put on some weight and looked older, more distinguished and definitely more handsome. He was aging well, like his father, who had been so good-looking even in his 50s, when Ayesha had last met him.

In her mind, she was transported back 15 years to the tarmac in that small town where she had gone to meet Shantanu—one last time. He had his hands in the pockets of his trousers, a blank expression on his face as he had watched her walk on the tarmac to the waiting airplane. And he had said nothing. Nothing to appease her, nothing to lessen her hurt. She had looked at him one last time, wanting to carry a last memory back with her.

Ayesha looked at his handsome face with a smile. 'Shantanu, you have not changed at all.' He winked at her, held her at an arm's distance, and said, 'And you are a teeny bit chubby, huh Ayesha.'

Chubby. The name he always called her though she was hardly chubby back then. Over the years, she had often wondered if it was a standard term he used with all the women he had pursued and won.

He held her hand as they walked into the coffee shop. The manager came bustling towards them—he knew Ayesha well. She would often come for meetings, or for a cup of coffee with her friends.

Sid always teased her about the fact that all the hotel managers and restaurant stewards knew her so well and were always fawning over her. Ayesha had a way with them. She remembered names without having to look at their name tags a second time, and she made it a point to remember a small, personal detail. Like with this manager who had come forward to greet them. Some months ago, he had had a bandage on his left hand and Ayesha asked him about it. He had hurt himself on the local train when a stone came flying through the window and hit his hand as he raised it to brush the hair off his face. Ayesha now said to him, 'Thank God you raised your arm. Else you could have so badly hurt your face.' It took so little to make people feel good about themselves, to make them feel like someone cared. And Ayesha always left a generous tip!

The manager took them to a nice little corner, away from the piano and the pianist who raised his arm to wave at Ayesha. Once they were comfortably settled in, the manager took their order—Shantanu ordered a double espresso, and Ayesha asked for her favorite, a hot toddy without rum. She loved the way they made the drink there. Loads of cinnamon, cloves, black pepper, ginger, lemon, and a generous dose of honey and nutmeg, in hot water.

A small smile played on Shantanu's face. 'So you still have not lost your popularity status with guys! Look at the guy fawning all over you.'

Ayesha laughed. 'Gosh, you remember?'

'Of course,' snorted Shantanu.' It was like being with royalty when we went out together. From the *vada pav* guy in front of Mithibai to the waiter at Mahesh Lunch Home. They all loved serving you.'

'I am the Goddess of the Working Class. Their fantasy,' she joked.

'Ya right!' he laughed.

Ayesha could not take her eyes off him. *Shit, he is just as I imagined him to be... sexy, suave. The idiot is so good-looking.*

'Admiring my 40-plus self?' interjected Shantanu.

—You did always read my mind well. Yup. You look really good. I bet the young bimbettes in your office drool over you.

—Ya I guess they do. I am their fantasy. A pot-bellied god with a receding hairline!

Ayesha shook her head, 'You are an ass. How did you get so elegant looking? Success sits easy on you, Shantanu.'

—How would you know anything about me?

—We have common friends, remember? You have done well—managing director of one of the largest and fastest-growing food chains in India! I thought you knew nothing apart from butter chicken and *naan*!

—I grew up. My taste buds expanded.

To accommodate flavors other than women.

—How are your parents?

—They are doing good. Still in Delhi, same old house. Though they do come to visit us and Nikhil.

—I saw them a few years ago when I was in Delhi. They were in my building block. And Shantanu, they didn't even recognize me. Thank god for that. I wouldn't have known what to say to them.

There was a lull as Ayesha looked down at her hands, fingering her wedding ring. The steward came back with their order and when he left Ayesha said matter-of-factly, 'Why did you call me? After all these years? What do you want?'

Shantanu looked at Ayesha's face. There was a smile hovering on her lips and some confusion in her eyes.

He said, 'I wanted to see you again. And see how you were doing.'

—After 15 years?

—I thought it was enough time to forget what had happened in the past. I have been meaning to reach out to you. I had never wanted to hurt you.

Really?? Was it that easy for him? I didn't want to hurt you—that must be one of the best-loved clichés in the world. It helped assuage his guilt, if any, and allowed him to move on with his life. I didn't mean to hurt you must in some manner nullify a karmic reaction.

Almost like Pilate—washing your hands off someone's pain and suffering. I didn't mean to hurt you was disowning responsibility for one's actions.

Shantanu looked ill at ease.

'I wanted to make sure you were okay. That you were doing fine Ayesha.'
Ayesha wondered how she was expected to respond now, 15 years
later.

I have been fine, for many years, even though I have pined for you
endlessly?

Or I took a long time to get over you and then returned to some sort
of normalcy?

Or that I have never opened my heart to someone after you bruised
it?

It had taken Ayesha a long, long time to shut her mind to the
horror of breaking up with Shantanu. Ritu, Shantanu's close
friend from college, had called her one day; Ayesha had met
Ritu at a party. When she asked to meet, Ayesha reckoned Ritu
was trying to be friends with her pal's girlfriend. There were no
mobile phones or emails those days, and since Shantanu was
stationed on a sales training stint in Rajkot, Ayesha thought she
would tell him about it at night when she called him. In the past
few weeks, Shantanu had stopped calling her and she called him
and wrote to him all the time. She didn't think too much about it.
She thought he was saving money and since she stayed at home with
her parents, it was no big deal for her.

Ayesha understood that day what people mean when they say
'it takes just a split second for your life to change'. That meeting with
Ritu changed her life. It made the ground beneath her feet shift and
shattered Ayesha.

Ritu did not smile or stand up to hug Ayesha as Ayesha walked
into the coffee shop. Ayesha thought that was a bit strange. When
she sat down, Ritu got straight to the point. She said Shantanu had
asked her to speak to Ayesha. That he did not want to be with her
anymore. He did not love her and his parents did not want him to
see her anymore.

Ayesha was taken aback. She retorted, 'And why would he tell you
that? Why would he not tell me himself?'

'He has been trying to tell you Ayesha, but you have not been listening to him. I am telling you all this because he is committed to marrying me.'

Marrying Ritu? Where did that come from?

Ayesha's mind started to seize up. 'But aren't you guys friends?'

'Yes we are', said Ritu. 'We've been friends since college and fell in love there too. Our parents have also met and want us to get married.'

Ayesha's temper got the better of her.

'So that coward sent you to do his dirty business. You know he has slept with me right?'

Ritu's tone became cold.

'Yes I know Ayesha. And what did you think? That you would sleep with him and he would marry you? Haven't you learnt better? Boys, especially Indian boys, don't marry the girls they sleep with.'

Ayesha was stunned. 'You know all this and you still want to marry him?'

Ritu shrugged her pretty shoulders and stated smugly. 'He is an attractive man, and can't help himself if women throw themselves at him, can he? He told me you came on to him one evening when you all went out together and he couldn't stop you. He went along with you. And that it happened just once, and that you have been chasing him ever since. I love him enough to forgive him that one time.'

Ayesha shut up. What could she say to a woman who loved Shantanu and was so blind to the truth in front of her? Could she tell her that Shantanu had pursued her for months till she had consented to sleep with him? That it was not once, but many stolen weekends when they both traveled on work? She knew every part of Shantanu's body. She knew how he tensed up and his eyes glazed over when he was about to come. She knew his favorite position—having her sit on top of him and moving them both in rhythm with their bodies slick with sweat. She knew how he tidied everything up after a love-making session. She knew how he smelt when he had a cold coming on. He liked taking a bath with piping hot water and took half a teaspoon of sugar in his tea.

She said nothing to Ritu. A part of her wanted to slap Ritu, and a part of her pitied the woman in front of her. Ayesha picked up her bag and said, 'I am sorry. This is all a big misunderstanding. Best of luck in your life together.'

That walk out of the coffee shop was the longest walk ever for Ayesha. She only prayed she would not stumble clumsily, as she always did, and that she would reach the safety of her car before making a fool of herself in front of Ritu.

How long did she sit in her car? Ayesha had no clue. Her brain had clamped down. Her eyes were dry. She sat there, thinking nothing. In the following days, all that Ayesha felt was hurt and betrayal. At some level, she wished Shantanu would call her and tell her it was all a joke. That he loved her.

Shantanu's voice brought her back from her thoughts. Here he was, sitting in front of her, looking at her with those eyes that used to melt her every single time. 'Hello. I asked you a question Ayesha.'

What kind of a man sends his fiancée to clean up his mess for him? And yet has the audacity to ask me to meet him after all this time.

Ayesha smiled and said, 'Life has been good to me Shantanu. Better than I would have ever expected. I got all that I wanted—a great husband, a good career, loving kids, and a great lifestyle. I have traveled the world and have, by and large, been happy. And you?'

Shantanu shrugged and said, 'So far so good! I have been out of India a lot. I have two kids and they keep us on our toes.'

'So you did marry Ritu at the end of it all.'

Shantanu had the grace to look a little embarrassed, and a little defensive. 'Yes Ayesha, but you know how it was with my parents. They had decided that they wanted me to marry her.'

Ayesha laughed, 'Oh please Shantanu. After so many years, shouldn't you be truthful to yourself at least? She is the one you loved, so why bring your parents into it? You wanted her, and not me. And you made your choice. I don't really feel bad anymore. When we were younger, the term "fuck buddies" had not been coined yet, so there was no name to give this relationship we shared. It took me a long time to understand it was purely sexual.'

Shantanu said, 'I know it must have been tough for you. I was away at Rajkot. Away from it all while you were stuck with all the friends and family. I just didn't know how to set things right.'

Easy to say that now.

Ayesha had shied away from all their friends. At work, she became withdrawn and always on the edge. No one could get in a word with her—it was like she was sitting on dynamite, ready to explode any moment. At home, she would escape to her room and read quietly. Her parents were furious with her when she told them she was done with Shantanu. She could not tell them what had transpired, and in any case, they had never quite liked him. They were angry because she had been so indiscreet in her love affair. And Indian society is unforgiving when it comes to marriage with a girl who has a romantic past. She had lost precious marriageable years with Shantanu and now her parents would have to begin the process of looking for a boy for her all over again.

Sleep eluded her. Her mind played out the showdown with Ritu, the lovemaking with Shantanu, the pitying looks in the eyes of her friends. She woke up clammy from her nightmares. In her dreams, Shantanu would come to her and then leave—and she would be distraught because she had lost his number, or because she couldn't find him and there was no way to contact him.

Crazily, she had loved him still. And almost made excuses for him. That he was caught between his parents, Ritu, and her. She wanted him—desperately—that is all she remembered.

Was there a point in telling him all this? Ayesha brooded. *I stopped mattering to him a long time ago, so why should he care any longer? He never thought to apologize to me—for betraying my trust, for making Ritu talk to me, for making me lose faith, self-esteem, and confidence. He never looked my way again.*

Ayesha smiled, 'It's all in the past now. It mattered for a while, but it doesn't anymore. At that time, I had thought I would never stop loving you, that you would come back to me telling me this was all a huge mistake, that you would be mine.

But you were never mine. Like you never belonged to any of the other friends you had sex with. I realized much later that those were your fuck buddies too—Natasha, Harmeet, Amrita. And they all must have been so heartbroken to see you with me. And then to lose you to Ritu.'

Shantanu's eyes never left Ayesha's face. She couldn't read what he was thinking. She had never been able to read his mind. When it became too disconcerting, Ayesha said, 'What? Why are you staring at me like that?'

Shantanu took his eyes off her face, and looked around the coffee shop. Ayesha noticed that the place had filled up since they had come in. She could see some people she knew sitting two tables away. From the likes of it, there was a story narration for a movie underway. Ayesha glanced at the other tables and thought—*there is a story for every one of the people sitting here. Some happy, some sad, but each life has its own share of ups and downs. Who would have thought I would meet Shantanu after so many years and have a civil conversation with him? This man, who caused me so much pain.*

Shantanu signaled to the steward to get him a refill. He looked at his phone and said, 'You know Ayesha, your face haunts me—the way you looked at me on that last day at the airport. It was a look of such disappointment that I never quite got over it. And I never mustered the courage to call you or meet you after that day.'

Ayesha remembered that weekend well. She had told her parents she had to go out for the weekend for a conference. They were not talking to her and did not question her.

Ayesha *had* to meet Shantanu one last time. She couldn't let him get away with the humiliation he had put her through. He did not take her calls anymore, telling his servant to tell her he was out or traveling. What kind of a person does that? Send a message for a break up through another person, and not speak to her even once? A coward is what he was, and she was going to force him to face her. She reached Rajkot and took a cab to his office. She had been there before, when she had visited Shantanu one weekend. She knew he was in town; it was the end of the month and he would be in the sales office, on the phone with his sales representatives, trying to close the month close to or above the budget.

When Shantanu saw her walking into the office, his face looked stricken. Ayesha stifled a hysterical laugh. *Did he really think I would not hit back? Had he forgotten what a firebrand I was reputed to be?* Then Shantanu's face changed. He whispered fiercely 'What are you doing here?'

'I need to talk to you.'

Ayesha was proud of herself. She was poised and while her heart thumped badly, there was no quaver in her voice. Her face was composed, and did not show her anxiety or fear.

Shantanu told her, 'Why don't you go home and wait for me?'

She looked at him defiantly, 'Why don't I sit here and wait for you to get done?'

'Have it your way. You know today is a bad day for me.'

And Shantanu got busy. Ayesha watched him as he cajoled, scolded, pampered and engaged with his sales officers on phone and in person. The office boy got her tea while she waited. She drank Shantanu in—she was furious with him, and yet he was a pleasure to watch at work. She hated him, and yet wanted to touch him. To feel him again. *What a slut I am. Wanting a guy who has rejected me with such complete humiliation.*

By the time he was done, it was almost 10 p.m. There was silence in the car as he drove them back home. Shantanu's servant was taken aback when he opened the door and saw her. For the past few weeks he had been making excuses for his master who did not want to speak to her. She saw his awkwardness and felt strange too, but managed a weak smile at him. Shantanu told him to lay the food and go back to his room. They would clean up later.

The mundane details of the evening were lost to her. All Ayesha remembered was choking on the food with anger and finally erupting on Shantanu. This was not the way she had planned to handle him. She had wanted to be calm and composed to tell him exactly what she thought of him. But she slammed her spoon down and said, 'Why? Why did you do what you did?'

'I did nothing,' said Shantanu, tucking into his food.

And Ayesha saw red. 'You are such a coward. You did nothing. Just sent in your girlfriend to clean up your mess and hid behind the bitch's skirt. If you have the audacity to fuck women with your cock, have the courage to tell them when it's over. And how dare you get your next woman in line to call me and tell me to back off? That's what your fancy parents taught their precious little son? Bastards all.'

—Don't get cheap Ayesha. I have been telling you. You just refuse to listen. I didn't tell Ritu to speak to you. She was home the weekend I was in Delhi and I told you to shut up on the phone because there was a parallel line. She heard everything.

—Oh wow Shantanu! You tell me now that she was home with you? You refused to meet me because you had a family dinner that night, remember? Fucking liar.

—Yes, it was a family dinner, dammit. Ritu's family had come over.

—Oh so she counts as family.

Ayesha could have slapped him. She thought she could murder him, and not mind spending a lifetime in the jail.

—You bastard! All this while that you have been fucking me, you have been planning your marriage with her!

Shantanu's face was red. And in his eyes Ayesha saw dislike and disgust. And it broke her. Her tears refused to stay in her eyes. She broke down.

—Why did you lead me up the garden path Shantanu? Only so you could get me into bed? Just another one of your conquests?

Shantanu was cold, 'I never promised you anything Ayesha. I always told you we were friends. I never ever said I would marry you.'

Maybe I had got it wrong, thought Ayesha. Maybe he had not said those words in the throes of passion. Maybe I misunderstood everything. Her head felt so muddled.

—I love you Shantanu. Totally, wholly, with my whole life. I can't believe you are throwing me out of your life.

—I am fond of you Ayesha. And that's all there has ever been. I can't keep you in my life Ayesha. Ritu won't allow it.

—You never told me the truth about Ritu. You told me she was your close pal.

—She is, Ayesha. And she is also the chosen one—my parents adore her. They have known her for years. She has always been with them even when I was out studying or working.

Ayesha put her head in her hands. 'You should have told me the truth about you two earlier Shantanu. I would not have made such a fool of myself. Shamed myself so.'

Shantanu said nothing. He went to her and held her. She let herself be held—all she wanted to do was melt away into nothingness. All the pain was so absurd. To have misread the situation, to have fallen in love with someone who did not care, the humiliation of loving him and losing him. The stupidity of the whole situation hit her. She felt him get hard against her.

Now, as Ayesha looked at Shantanu across the table, she thought about that last time they made love. *Break-up sex, isn't that what they call it these days? I can't remember if I enjoyed it. I remember crying through it the whole time. I had not wanted the moment to end, did not want to lose him and could think of nothing but Shantanu.* She smiled. Shantanu looked at her quizzically and raised an eyebrow. She used to try and copy him, but could never manage to raise one eyebrow like he did.

—I was just thinking that you were an adept young lover Shantanu. It took me a while to realize that it was all because of your sweet 'girlfriends' like me. We gave you so much practice.

Shantanu's mask was back in place. Ayesha knew that look well. It meant: 'Don't mess with me'.

The last time they made love—Ayesha woke up feeling cold and clammy against Shantanu. He was fast asleep. She looked at him for a long while and then got up and went to the bathroom. She took a long shower and scrubbed her body again and again. She wanted his smell off her face, off her body.

When she got out of the bathroom, Shantanu was up. With his hands behind his head, calmly lying down on the bed, his eyes followed her. She said nothing. She wore her clothes. When she was brushing her hair, he came up behind her and nuzzled his face into her hair. She smacked him hard on his cheek. Shantanu stepped back in surprise and said, 'Whoa, what happened?'

Ayesha looked at him. She felt cold. Cold with a white anger. The kind of anger that comes with a calmness in your heart. It allowed her to tell him exactly what she thought of him. It gave her courage—to move the blame from herself and park it in the place it deserved to rest. It gave her the courage to leave without shaming herself anymore.

And she said, 'You are a slut Shantanu. And you will put your cock anywhere, in any woman, with no regard for anyone's feelings. I am glad you chose Ritu. She can marry her whore and think she got a prize catch.'

Shantanu had the grace to say nothing.

'You ruined my life. Systematically. Deliberately. All for sex. You made me fall in love with you. You flaunted me among friends, all the time aware that you were only using me. All for a romp in bed? People might look at me and pity me. And say, "Here is the poor thing who Shantanu used and dumped". Well, good for them. I know I did it for love, so I am not ashamed. You are actually worse than any whore anywhere. Whores at least have the moral values of being honest in their expectations and reasons.

I pity Ritu. For thinking she has a decent guy, when all she really caught was a gigolo.'

And with that, Ayesha had left. As she walked out of his house, Shantanu ran after her and said, 'Where are you going?'

Without looking at him she said, 'You are dropping me off at the airport.'

Numbness is what Ayesha had felt. She looked out of the window for the entire ride, absorbing nothing, waiting to get back home. Waiting to hug her mom and waiting to sleep in her bed. Waiting for this time to pass by.

Now, Ayesha looked at Shantanu across the table and wondered if this was the guy she had mooned over for so many years. He was good-looking, yes, elegant too. But he had none of the gentleness and grace that Sid had. She liked the way Sid looked. The way he smiled. His charm. His sense of humor. His integrity. His commitment to her. Shantanu just did not match up.

We women can be so crazy. When a guy dumps us, we lose all perspective about ourselves. Go through so much heartbreak and think we will never love again. What a load of crap. Imagine if I had married Shantanu—I would have been an emotional wreck worrying who he was sleeping with. Once a slut, always a slut.

Shantanu breathed in deep and said.

'We were young Ayesha. And I was a prick. A typical spoilt *Punju* boy. Brash. It took me years to understand how much pain I must have caused you.'

'Well, here you are. Apologizing 15 years later. If it rankled you for a decade and a half, I would say I got my revenge,' smiled Ayesha.

'Sometimes I wish I had not left you Ayesha. That last look has haunted me for the longest time. I failed you. But I was shaken by the whole thing too. Ritu and my parents on one side and you on the other. I could not make the choice. I know you don't believe me, but in my own stupid, demented way, I loved you too. And now I don't want to let go of you—ever.'

Ayesha said, 'Stop Shantanu. Please don't. Tell me something— have you told Ritu you are meeting me today?'

Shantanu fell silent.

'Then there is no scope for us to be friends. I will always love you Shantanu. Not in the having-an-extramarital-affair-with-you kind of way. But you were special to me, and I retain that in a part of my heart. But I don't want you in my life any longer.'

The evening transformed for Ayesha. All that she had felt was off her chest now and she felt a lightness in her being. As she watched the glorious sunset over the Arabian sea from where she sat in the coffee shop, Ayesha sent a silent thanks to her parents who had stood by her, to Sid who loved her for all she was, for the wonderful life she had.

It turned out to be a great, comfortable evening. Shantanu and

Ayesha spoke about many things as the evening wore on. About common friends, marriage, parents and kids. They chatted about the stupid things they had done together, the fun they'd had, till they slept together and the relationship went through a drastic transformation. Ayesha's mind frequently wandered off. She thought of Sid, her gorgeous Sid. Who she met through her parents, and liked immediately. The day she had told him about Shantanu, Sid had held her gently and caressed her hair and kissed her as she wept out her hurt. Slowly and steadily, he had worked like a balm on her wounds, and helped her heal. And through the years, he never questioned when she woke up from her nightmares about Shantanu. He knew, and would only hold her tight and lull her back into sleep. She thought of Sid's love for her, the kind that said: 'I am here for you and I will always protect you'.

Ayesha felt Shantanu's hold over her heart slip away. She had longed for him and missed him—or had it been the idea of that elusive love that had appealed to her so?

There were more precious things waiting for her back home. A family that she had created with the husband she now realized she deeply loved. A husband who made her secure in his love for her and whom she took for granted in her life.

Ayesha looked at the time. It had been almost three hours. The crowd around them had changed. The corporate crowd had been replaced by diners out for the evening, waiting in the coffee shop for family and friends to arrive and then proceed to one of the restaurants in the hotel. It was dark outside now, and she knew her driver would be getting worked up—it was way past his official hour. Ayesha picked up her bag, 'I really need to go Shantanu. It is nearing nine, and I have to get dinner organized for my kids. Sid must be home now too.'

Shantanu stood up reluctantly and hugged her. 'I always cared for you, you know that right Ayesha?'

Ayesha looked at him and kissed him on the cheek, 'Yes, I do...and thanks for dumping me Shantanu. That was the best gift you ever gave me!'

She walked out with a spring in her step. This time, she did not turn back to see Shantanu standing there, looking at her. Sure, she liked Shantanu still, was even fond of him, but she had finally achieved closure and could get on with the business of living without him. He would haunt her no more!

Veera

I am back in our courtyard in Rawalpindi before the Partition uprooted me from the only home I had ever known. It was a cold, crisp winter day. It must have been mid-morning or late afternoon because the men had all left for work.

We were sitting in the courtyard in front of our rooms—all the rooms opened into the central courtyard. My grandmother, *baaji*, my mother, *beyji*, my aunts, my cousins, and some ladies from the neighboring houses. We must have had a community hair wash, because all of us girls were getting oil put in our hair. *Beyji* used coconut oil, which used to be frozen white in the winters.

She would put it outside in the sun and wait for it to melt. I loved mustard oil, its pungent fragrance, but *beyji* used only coconut oil in my hair. She used to massage me with mustard oil when I was much younger. All of us young girls were getting our hair braided into tight plaits that were tied up with a ribbon. My ribbon was blue that day. *Bauji*, which was how I addressed my father, had got it for me from Peshawar when he had gone there on work the previous week. The air was redolent with the smells of groundnuts and oranges and the ground was littered with groundnut shells and orange peels. The festival of *Lohri* was round the corner. Each year, all the neighbors got together to set up a large bonfire at the end of the street on this day. The servants would bring in the firewood and one of the older men would supervise the construction of the bonfire. If Jagat *Chacha* was getting it done, the bonfire would be short and stout like him. If Raja *Chacha* was in-charge, the bonfire would be tall and narrow. I preferred Jagat *Chacha's* arrangement; the fire didn't seem so scary and all around the bonfire, we would set up *charpoys* for everyone to sit. Each house brought something for the bonfire and the dinner thereafter. There was *revadi* and *gajak*, made with *gud*, not sugar as you get in the markets now, and groundnuts, corn kernels, and *chidva*. The older ladies would sing songs as we all went around the fire. As we threw in the offerings, we would all say a little prayer that had a wish in it too. (That year, I wished for a new red bag to take to school.)

I have forgotten the songs now, though I do remember the legend of Dulla Bhatti, the brave son of Punjab who refused to recognize the Mughal Akbar as his emperor. Apart from fighting the Mughal forces, Dulla Bhatti also protected the young Hindu and Sikh girls from the Mughal forces, getting them married and organizing dowries for them. Lots of our songs were about Dulla Bhatti. While the men sat around gossiping and drinking, the women would also chat, sing and prepare dinner.

Every year, *baaji* would set up the *tandoor*. The servant boy would give her the dough balls and she would expertly pat them into the most delicious *rotis* and *naans*. I never saw her burn her hand when she put the dough in the *tandoor* to make the bread. And when she took it out, *beyji* or one of the other women would put a large dollop of white butter on it. Till today, I can feel the softness of the *naan* and the hot melted butter on my tongue. I am a good cook and have eaten my share of different cuisines, but nothing is as tasty as *baaji's* dishes. My favorite meal at *Lohri* was *sarson ka saag* and *makkai ki roti* with dollops of white butter. And of course, *gajar ka halwa*, with lots of *khoya* and nuts.

When I started my catering business, my *sarson ka saag* was very popular. And my secret ingredient was quite simply the fact that I never added spinach or any other greens to it. I made the *saag* with only mustard greens. Just the way *baaji* made it.

That sunny, cold afternoon, the ladies were talking about the partition of India. The Muslims were lobbying for a separate homeland after independence from England, because they would never feel comfortable staying with Hindus in 'Hindustan'. Everywhere in Rawalpindi, the adults could be heard discussing our independence from the British and what would happen after that. What would go to the Hindus and what would the Muslims get?

Baaji was a sharp old woman. I still remember bits of the conversation.

Someone said, 'What will happen to us Sikhs? Who knows what part of Punjab will come under the new country. My brothers migrated to Lyallpur 15 years ago to farm in the canal colonies. So many Sikhs have gone there. Will that go to the new country? Will we have to leave Rawalpindi?'

Another woman: '*Baaji*, will they also give Sikhs some land?'

To which *baaji* responded, '*Arre kamli*. Who will consider us separate from the Hindus? All of us have Hindu and Sikhs in the same family. Look at us. *Sardarji* was the oldest son in his family. He was gifted to the Sikh religion and Guru Nanak. All the others in his family are Hindus. How will anyone separate Hindus and Sikhs?'

Beyji said, 'How can we leave Rawalpindi? This is our home!'
Baaji replied, 'Let it be *bibi*. We have no control over these things.
Let's see what happens? *Sardarji* was telling me that he is sending
jewelry to our relatives in Delhi. If anything happens, at least we will
have something to start afresh with.'
'Namo is pregnant. How will she travel?'
Baaji finally put a stop to the discussion. '*Chhaddo ji*. Why are we
getting tense when nothing is certain?'
I was not worried. There was much on my mind. One of my cousins
had seen Simmi, a neighbor's daughter, going alone in the fields.
She had been doing it every afternoon, once all the ladies were done
with their work, and either catching a nap, or sunning themselves
and gossiping. She would be dressed in her best clothes, with *kajal*
in her eyes and a nice *parandi* in her hair. My cousin swore that
Simmi smelled different too. She was always humming a song and
looked very happy. Speculation was rife that she was meeting the
handsome *jawan* Jaswant who was home on holidays from the
army. We were all itching to sneak out and spy on Simmi.
I was six at the time. No one in our days used to remember dates. If
you asked anyone when they were born, you would get varied answers. 'I was born the year it was so hot that all the wells had dried
up.' Or 'I was born when the watermelons were in full bloom'. Or 'I
was born the year the carnival came to the village'.
I know the year I was born and my age too. Simply because
Veerji, my oldest brother, elder to me by 12 years, kept our dates.
The English master at school told him that it was 'native' to not do
so. Veerji wanted to be like the British who ruled us. He loved their
language and would try and imitate the way the master walked,
talked, and conducted himself. So in an attempt to not be 'native' he
decided to record all our births.
There were so many of us in that house. Father, his three brothers,
and their families all stayed in the sprawling *haveli* at Rawalpindi.
In my mind, I can still clearly see the wall in the kitchen where
Veerji made a note of all our births. It was sooty, black and unclean,
and over time, Veerji got into a lot of trouble with *bauji* because he

refused to let anyone clean it or paint it over. He was *beyji's* darling and got away with it, because the kitchen was her domain.

I hear 'Mom' being said and struggle to return.

It is Piya's voice. And she is talking to KD about me.

—*Bhai*, it has been over a week. Mom is not responding. I don't know how much longer this will take.

—Can't say. The doctors say it could happen any time; it could take days or she can come out of the coma even now.

—I feel horrible when I imagine that Mom fell down in her bathroom and no one realized until morning that she had passed out on the bathroom floor. What must she have gone through?

—It isn't anyone's fault Piya. We check on her through the night even though she has that dumb nurse who slept through it all.

—I am not accusing you KD. Why are you taking it so personally? I am merely thinking out loud that it must have been horrible for her.

—It's your stupid tone Piya.

—No *bhai*. I can't stop thinking that Mummy must be so lonely. I know we all love her and are there for her, but she does not have anyone her age anymore. I dread the thought of being lonely.

In that house in Rawalpindi, there was no concept of loneliness. There were always so many of us kids. *Beyji* had three kids. Veerji who was 12 years older, then Nimmi who was six years older than me. I hung around with my cousin, Channi, who was three months older than me. I don't remember very clearly now, but I think we were about 20 of us in all.

Dinnertime was the only time we were all together. In the day, some of us went to school and the older boys went to work with the men. We were traders in oil and spices and there was plenty of work for the boys. After the fourth standard, the girls stopped going to school and helped in the house. And got married fairly young. Nimmi got married when I was five, so that means she was 11. She got her period when she was 11 years old.

According to tradition, while girls got married at a young age, they stayed with their parents till they got their period. Then the girl would leave for her marital home. I remember when Nimmi left. She had many trunks full of clothes, jewelry, linen, utensils and gifts for her new family. We young kids were excited and the older women were sad as they prepared to send her off.

In our room I heard *beyji* crying and talking to *bauji*, 'What does an 11-year-old know about marriage, or the marital bed, or adjusting to a new family? Before Nimmi has even grown up, she will become a stranger to this family and be part of a family where the son will always comes first.'

Bauji tried to console her, 'Don't get so sad. You also came to this family so young. Are you not taken care of? Have you and I not grown up together?'

'Yes *ji*, but we don't know how good they will be to Nimmi. When you go to leave her, will you tell *behenji* that Nimmi can't sleep in the dark? And that she likes milk with tea leaves in it? She can read and write Urdu and Punjabi so will they consider letting her continue her studies? Also, if they will let her visit next summer?'

Bauji hugged *beyji*, 'Okay *bhagyawan*, I will tell her mother-in-law all that. Now wipe your tears. We need to do *ardaas* before we leave.'

Beyji hugged Nimmi a lot that day and fussed over all the meals. She made all the things Nimmi liked and also packed *besan laddoos* for her. Veerji gave Nimmi envelopes with stamps on them so she could write to us every week. The house seemed so empty for a few days after Nimmi left.

Dinnertime in the Rawalpindi *haveli* was fun. We all had to wash up and go and sit on the *chattais* on the floor. *Baaji* sat in one corner, on her small stool, watching us with a hawk's eye. God forbid if any of the neighbors told her of the pranks we had played that day, because that would mean a round of ear pulling. Those thin scrawny hands had a lot of strength in them.

Once we were fed and our chores were done, *baaji* would hold court. Her stories were magnificent. I can still see her sitting on that string bed in the courtyard, with a big brass glass of water on a stool next to her. She loved water, and would sip all day from her big brass *churriwala* glass. I loved those big glasses. *Beyji* had promised me one when I was slightly older. All of us had smaller brass tumblers with our names etched on them. Each day, one of the younger ones was assigned to keep refilling her glass. Any failure or tardiness meant a sharp pull of the braids or the *judi* for the boys and a smack on the ear.

When KD's son Ranvir was younger, he would ask me to tell them stories. And he loved the stories of Rawalpindi. I would tell him the stories *baaji* told us. His favorite one was about the *chudail* who had been troubling a nearby village. For many weeks, the traders had refused to come to the village and the men refused to cross the forest that separated it from the next village. The *chudail* had put the fear of the devil in everyone. Those who had seen her said that the *chudail* wore white robes and had red eyes. Her hair was long and matted. She had talons instead of hands and her feet were turned inward. She would attack passers-by and take away their money and belongings, all the while chanting some black magic spell. She knew most of the people she had robbed by name. The villagers were too scared to go there.

And now comes my favorite part. My grandfather went to the forest on his big black stallion. When the *chudail* appeared, he caught her by her hair. She started shrieking loudly, begging to be released.

When grandfather tore her white robe from her body, she fell at his feet and started pleading for mercy. Grandfather got down from his horse and picked her up. He realized she was a woman from their village. Her husband had gone to the city and wed another woman. This poor woman was left alone to fend for her three small children and herself in the village. She thought extorting money like this was the best way for her to earn some money. *Baaji* said that grandfather gave her back her white robe and did not tell anyone about the incident. From that day, our family supported her family, and one of her sons was employed in our trading business.

There were so many more stories. How my mother always saved me a big chunk of butter for my *parantha*. How we sucked on sugarcane and *ganeris* in season. How we stole mangoes from the farms near our house. How we continued to eat raw guavas despite the stomach aches at night. How we once threw the dog in the well in the garden just to see him flail desperately and howl. What a hiding we got that day from our fathers! They were furious that the dog would have died if the gardener had not got there on time. How the *dhobi's* daughter hated to sleep in her house because her father snored so loudly. So she would sneak into our room and sleep near the door. And be gone before any of the mothers came in the morning. How we used to go to the fields to relieve ourselves and had to be careful that no snake came out at the time. How we found Simmi and Jaswant Singh in the fields and hid their clothes behind the sugarcane. Then we sat on the path back to the village and waited for them. They both came out looking very sheepish and refused to meet our eyes. And how Veerji was angry because the *bhaiji* at the gurudwara refused to give him *parshad* the fourth time. Next time the *bhaiji* went to the fields to relieve himself, Veerji lit a firecracker under his butt. The *bhaiji* got the scare of his life, and a burnt butt. And Veerji almost got scalped for the prank and it took all the women of the house to save him from my father. Everything you do becomes a story in your life. Some of these stories exist only in your mind. They are difficult to narrate. These are the ones that trouble you the most, because even if you want to, you can't share them.

Loneliness. You don't know what it does to you. Back in Rawalpindi, had anyone told me that I would be lonely one day, I would have laughed at their face and thought they were sprinkling salt on my wounds. I used to crave solitude those days. And there was none to be had. You got slapped by your mother? There would be an audience watching your shame. You got your period? All the women, the children, and the maids, and possibly even the fathers were aware of it. You wanted to cry? No empty room!

There was no way you could be lonely in that Rawalpindi *haveli*.

Namita

To: Piyar@gmail.com
From: namitap@gmail.com
Jun 21, 2013
8 p.m.

Stop going hysterical on me Piya. During the day, I don't get a signal in the trekking areas where I am shooting. Remember I told you about this shoot—the off-beat trekking trails near Karjat? I don't get a signal till I reach Karjat.

Just got in and got a barrage of mails and messages from you and KD. Has there been any improvement in her situation? What do the doctors say?

To: namitap@gmail.com
From: Piyar@gmail.com
Jun 21, 2013
8.05 p.m.

Sorry sis. Of course you had told me about the shoot. In this whole mess I forgot about it. Mom is still in a coma. The doctors think that because of the fall, an aneurysm in her brain burst. The first time I have heard of Glasgow Coma Scale, Namita. Apparently, it measures responses on eye, motor and verbal abilities. Mom is unreceptive on all.

We have all been in the hospital since morning, getting doctor appointments, figuring out which tests need to be conducted, if surgery is advisable for her and how to handle all this.

It is such a shocker. And Mom looks so small, almost like a baby. Her face is peaceful and I keep expecting her to open her eyes.

When are you heading back to Mumbai? You better come here soon. We need you.

To: Piyar@gmail.com
From: namitap@gmail.com
Jun 21, 2013
8.30 p.m.

Oh, she got hurt that bad? This is serious. Any idea how long this will take? I will split the hospital bills—tell KD that.

The shoot is on for another week, so I will be back in Mumbai then.

To: namitap@gmail.com
From: Piyar@gmail.com
Jun 21, 2013
9.00 p.m.

Are you serious Nami? Who said anything about money and hospital bills? And can't you leave your shoot and come? Namita, she is our mother. Who knows which way this may go?

To: namitap@gmail.com
From: Piyar@gmail.com
Jun 22, 2013
7.30 a.m.

So you don't want to respond huh?

To: Piyar@gmail.com
From: namitap@gmail.com
Jun 22, 2013
11 p.m.

Piya

I have been thinking about Mom all day. And I know you think I am wrong, but I have tried hard to get some positive emotion for her. I am feeling bad for her, hooked up in the hospital and unresponsive. I feel no love for her, and even now, all I have is a huge amount of anger against her.

I know it is difficult for you to understand me. I have lived with the feeling of being unloved for too long. In that house, all she cared about was KD. Her boy, her knight in shining armor. KD could do no wrong. All the goodies were reserved for KD. How many times did she not give me milk because she wanted to give it to her beloved son? She sold her precious gold bangles to get some money to send him to Harvard for his MBA. And she was furious when I asked her for some money so I could buy a camera? And once KD started doing well, she latched herself on to him completely. As if she was the reason he had become successful.

Hell, she didn't even care about Dad. You were too young then, but she used to ignore him completely. Sure, she gave him food, washed and ironed his clothes, and kept a clean house. But she never had a conversation with him. It was almost as if he did not exist. He was a shadow, hovering on her periphery. He is the one who helped her set up her business, and keep *maaji* off. She was polite to him, but so indifferent. I used to feel so bad for Dad. And when he died, she changed into this social butterfly...out every day, enjoying herself. She disgusts me. Parasite is what she is.

Mana

'Dear New Mrs. Kapoor,
I hope you have a cunt. If you do, please ensure that your husband
sticks his cock into it. And gets off my wife. Else it will not bode well
for him—or you.'
I was a new bride, all of three weeks. Recently returned from my
honeymoon—that silly term used to describe a 'getting-to-know'
holiday whose sole purpose is to discover your husband's body, let him
explore yours, and to begin to know the person your parents decided
you had to marry. It amazes me till today. When we were growing
up, we were supposed to stay away from boys. Not look at them, not

talk to them, let alone be friends with them. Then one fine day, they marry you to someone you don't know at all, and he has all the rights over your body. They even add sexy lingerie in your trousseau, and well-meaning aunties try to tell you how to 'perform'.

I was horrified to receive such a letter. I had not heard such words being said to me—ever. In the protected environment at my parents', no one abused. Even words like 'shit' or 'bitch' were not used. I didn't know what to make of the letter. I did not know KD, my husband of three weeks, all that well. Would he get angry? Would my marriage be over? I would certainly not be welcomed back into my parents' house, as conservative as that was. Where women were supposed to be seen, not heard. Where you had to sleep on a thin mattress on the days you had your period and could not enter the kitchen, so everyone knew your humiliation. I was too new in this household and did not want to be isolated. I did not want to offend and did not want to be sent back to my parents.

I was not KD's first choice. He did not even see me properly before we got married. In fact, we did not even get to talk on the phone, let alone go out. My parents did not want disaster to strike again.

The first time I set my eyes on KD, he had not come to meet me as a prospective groom. He had come to see my cousin, Geeta, who had just finished college and wanted to be a teacher. KD's family was progressive and did not mind the girl studying or working.

There were so many of us girls, and we had strict instructions to not come in front of the family. It would be a disaster if the boy chose any of us over Geeta. We were used to this drama and loved the whole intrigue.

So the day KD came, my cousins and I crouched in the balcony above to get a glimpse of the boy. He got out of his Maruti, wearing a blazer and blue jeans, with his mother and an uncle in tow. He looked intimidating, intelligent, intense. Like all IIT-Harvard types. We were used to the boys in our college who dressed funky, and had a cigarette or *bidi* in their mouths while they espoused lofty ideals that would change the world. They had the affected swagger of people who thought they owned the world. They were coveted as boyfriends, but were not husband material. KD was a league apart, one that you aspired to marry, but did not know how to get through to. Geeta was lucky. I didn't think I would ever marry such a guy.

After weeks, the matchmaking talks fell through. KD's mother was a small, sprightly thing, very observant. Apparently she did not think much of Geeta. My cousin was heartbroken and cried copiously for weeks.

Now married to KD, I did not know what to do. I could not call my brother and tell him what had happened. I fretted and fumed in my room. I cried and cried. KD's mother, Mom, as everyone called her, was worried. She came into my room and asked me why I had said no to lunch. Was something bothering me? Was I missing home? Did I want to go visit my parents? Had KD said something? She would take him to task if he had troubled me. I didn't know her so well either. Would she listen to anything against her beloved son? He was the star of the Kapoor *khandaan*.

I remember the day my parents told me they had fixed my marriage. I had expected it, of course. My family was not the kind who would encourage me to study more; taking up a job was unheard of. According to them, our future depended on our in-laws. If they wanted, I could study further, work, do whatever my in-laws 'allowed' me to do. Even before I had finished grade 12, my parents had started to look for respectable families and their eligible boys to get me married to.

But when they told me KD was the guy I was to marry, I was horrified. I threw a tantrum. Did they not know he had rejected Geeta? Yes, of course they did. But good guys are hard to come by and they had approached his family separately and asked if they would be interested in me. This time, KD did not even want to see the girl he was to marry. His mother consented. He said yes.

And I railed against the injustice. What was the big deal about this marriage? How could any guy have been so important that my family was willing to risk the wrath of Geeta's family?

In the end, I could not keep the humiliation to myself. When KD came home, he came directly to the bedroom. Mummy must have told him I was distraught and inconsolable. He came into the room, face awash with concern and held me. I felt revulsion. Like there were ants crawling on my skin. I threw the much-read letter, crumpled and soaked in my tears, on his face. 'This is what I get for becoming Mrs. Kapoor? The information that you are seeing other women? Why KD?'

The smoothness of the man I had married. He looked at the letter without a trace of guilt or emotion on his face and brushed it off. 'That is not for me. Someone must have sent it by mistake.'

'Really?' I told him. 'It has your name.'

He started kissing my tears. 'Someone must be playing a prank, my love. Why would I play around with someone's wife when I have this gorgeous thing next to me? Don't you trust me?'

Oh how I cried. And he sat down next to me consoling me, cuddling me, kissing me. And telling me it was a terrible misunderstanding. That he was feeling angry that someone would have the gall to play such a prank. He swore to find the miscreant and beat the hell out of that person.

Eventually, I let it pass. I was still young. I believed in love, in marriage. In KD.

My mother-in-law adores the ground KD walks on. I have heard KD's family saga from Mom so many times that I can narrate it in my sleep. Of how the family lost everything in the Partition and fled to Mumbai. How rich they were as landlords in Punjab and were left with nothing. How KD's father made do on a paltry salary in that little one-bedroom apartment on Chimbai Lane and led a miserable existence. How their fortunes changed with KD doing so well at work.

KD is driven. He wanted to rise above his station, to restore his family to its former glory so he studied hard. Getting into IIT was a big deal, and a sure ticket to future success. Since there was no money to pay for extra classes for IIT-JEE, KD started taking tuitions in maths and physics to pay for his extra classes. He got into

IIT, the first one on Chimbai Lane to have done so, and became a role model to the kids he tutored. The Chimbai Lane kids wanted to become like KD *bhaiyya*. And then KD went to Harvard, on a full scholarship, to do his MBA and hit pay dirt.

I molded myself into the ideal corporate wife. I learnt how to dress like a successful man's wife, learnt to soak up all the news around me so I could talk intelligently on issues. I learnt to entertain and drink socially, becoming the wife that would make KD proud. Mom involved me in her business, and together, Piya, she and I have made it successful. Mom has moved away from it, but she is invaluable. She is well known, and has great knowledge of all cuisines. I love her deeply, and admire the grit of this woman who has worked hard to beat her circumstances.

Yet, I lack.

TS Eliot is right—April is the cruelest month of them all. All of a sudden, the cool Mumbai 'winter' is over, and the humidity hits you smack in your face. The humid smells of unwashed bodies, sweat mingled with not fully dried clothes, assail the nose. Even in fancy Pali Hill, the stench can get overwhelming, the smell of drying fish on Danda and the putrid smells from the sea during low tide. The evening also brings no succor. Humidity makes the clothes cling to your body, no amount of anti-perspirants can mask the sweat in the underarms and the hair goes all frizzy and unmanageable.

Yet, Mumbai never stops partying. Good for our business, as Mom says. I am trying to set the menu for a movie director's party. His movie has just crossed the ₹100 crore mark and he wants to throw a success party for over 200 people. The bad news is that most of the swish Mumbai crowd is always on a diet— and most of them eat their salads and diet foods and come for these parties that begin only post 11 p.m. The good news for us is that the host still wants a lavish spread. His wife wants a French spread.

I am not sure if this small-town girl from Uttar Pradesh knows the difference between Awadhi and Mughlai cuisine, but who am I to argue. She wants French, she shall have French. The director's wife shall have French with dishes that have exotic-sounding names. I think artichoke tartlets, basil palmiers, éscargot-stuffed mushrooms, and Pâté Forestier should be good for appetizers. Blueberry balsamic chicken, broccoli and chives tarts, a cheese soufflé and confit byladi will suffice for the main course.

Mom is amused at such pretentiousness. When she started her business, she did what Piya and I call 'comfort foods'—*samosas, chhole bhature, puri aloo* and *papdi chaat*. Now most fancy parties shy away from such food. After all, foie gras sounds more exotic than butter chicken, and the Swiss raclette evokes more elegance than the good old Hyderabadi *biryani*. Well! who are we to complain? Our margins are huger than before!

In our plush Samshiba apartment at Pali Hill, the windows are open in the late evening. It is humid and hot, but I don't want the children to become used to air-conditioning all the time. I sit on the dining table and do my work. From my vantage position I can see the whole house. And the lights of Pali Hill apartments. I wonder what goes on in each of those apartments. Back in my parent's middle-class house in a middle-class Dadar colony, you could peep into neighbors' houses. Everyone knew what was happening in the other house. My mother used to constantly compare us to the neighbors' children who were supposedly studying all the time. At this time of the evening, the smells of food would fill the air. *Sambar* at the south Indian aunty's house, chicken or egg curry at the Parsi aunty's, the smell of *tadka* on the *toor dal* somewhere, the irresistible aroma of *rotis* and the hiss of the pressure cooker. To send someone a bowl of your house's specialty was such a done thing. The aunty upstairs loved the *rajma* that my mother made—the typical Punjabi kind. And we used to get *undhiyo* from the *Gujju* aunty in the winters, or *dhansak* from the Parsi aunty. And mother's best friend, Sudha Aunty always called me home for *idlis* and *dosas* because she knew I loved them.

Pali Hill is antiseptic. You seldom know your neighbors; in fact, it is advisable to not get too friendly with them. In these upmarket apartments there is always a fight brewing—over society matters, parking, and driver and maid problems. Someone gets whores home, or there is money laundering happening somewhere. We have a large group of friends and our neighbors are not part of any group. I miss those simpler times, when you could walk into your neighbor's and chat with them over a cup of tea. When your best friend stayed in the house next door, and there was never a dull evening.

I miss that life for my children. Now when they want to spend time with their friends after school, I have to set play dates. And those only fructify if children have time from the various post-school classes they go to. Piya and I joke sometimes that there is more money and less hassle in the kids' business. Art and craft, general knowledge, science, English, robotics, fitness for kids—the possibilities are endless. I feel bad for the children; they lead such structured lives. Though, as a mother, and a working one at that, it is perfect for my schedule.

The kids are in their room, just back from swimming, and finishing up their homework. The maid has taken them their milk and fruit. They are arguing about who gets to see their choice of program on TV first. I love the sounds of my children, even if they are fighting. They fill up the spaces in my heart and remind me why I continue to stay in this marriage.

While I plan the menu, I wait. For the laws of nature to balance themselves out. For *karma* to serve up just desserts. For deliverance from KD's never-ending infidelity.

Jealousy is an old hag. She nags you and nags you and cunningly makes you look at things from another crueler perspective. She does not stop, until you scream out loud, or do something you never intended to do. Then she sits back, nods her head in satisfaction, and waits for the next event to take place.

Jealousy is like a worm that finds its way into your innards. It bites, it nibbles, it eats, it erodes your insides. It causes pain—real physical pain. It makes you hollow; it makes you want to stop eating; it makes you want to eat; it makes you want to throw up.

Jealousy is like a volcano. It simmers and festers. It waits for a crack to show up and then gushes forth to the surface. In doing so, it burns up the insides, and then annihilates all that lies in its wake.

Jealousy is like fire. It burns and burns. It overwhelms the senses and it destroys. It wreaks havoc on the emotional landscape and leaves destruction in its wake. It destroys feelings of self-esteem, of self-respect.

Jealousy is like dry ice. It is cold and conniving. It makes you behave in ways you never thought possible and it makes you see yourself in a light you may not like. It makes you unlovable to yourself.

I tell myself that I have to stop caring. I have to stop being jealous. It has been 15 years and I keep jealousy next to me like an old trusted friend. She destroys me and refuses to let me go. I train hard. I chant, I pray, and I vent to my best friend. Yet, the moment KD, my husband of 15 years, walks into the house, she rears up inside of me. And makes me ugly. She gives me anger, so intense that I find myself wanting to hide myself from it. A hurt so deep cuts me like a knife that I struggle to smile. A feeling I want to throw up, and throw out all these horrible feelings.

Yet I keep quiet. I have been brought up to be a good Indian wife. A good Indian mother. A good Indian daughter and a good daughter-in-law. I cannot show these feelings and ruin the peace in my house.

No matter how well we are doing in life today, the fact is that we are strictly middle class. Separation, divorce—these things are not part of our social fabric. I have to take the bad things in my stride. Where will I go anyway? With two kids? And there is no guarantee that my future will be any brighter. At least I am Mrs. Kapoor. And have a great home and in-laws. Those are the only good things in this sham of a marriage.

KD is on the phone as he walks in, discussing the next week's product launch. He will begin traveling across the country from next week. He is not happy with the campaign, and thinks the distribution is going too slow. Rishika bounds up to him and hugs him tight. The pint-sized 10-year-old is the only one who can interrupt him on an official call. He hangs up the phone and takes her into a big bear hug. Ranvir walks up to him and KD ruffles his hair. I count till five; that is all it takes for KD and Ranvir to get into an argument. And on my count of five they do.

I look at KD—him with the salt-pepper hair, a toned body that is the result of an early morning run and a dedicated personal trainer. He looks distinguished in his Armani suit. He is the kind of guy you see in a five-star hotel lobby and think, 'This guy has arrived.' He is educated, successful, charming, suave—the kind of husband other women envy. The kind of guy whose attention women want.

I watch him being moralistic with the kids. And I wonder at his hypocrisy. He gets ticked off at Ranvir because Ranvir contradicts him. The boy is all of 13 and at the very nascent stage of teenage temper tantrums. KD riles him with his constant criticism. Ranvir's marks are never good, he should have a better position in the football team, he spends too much time on his devices, he is putting on weight, his friends are a bad influence...the list of negatives is endless. Can KD, this bigshot who is featured in business magazines every other month for being the most successful entrepreneur in recent years, not see his foolhardiness? He will lose Ranvir with his stupid behavior. Sometimes I wish I could badmouth him to the kids, and turn them against him. But a part of me stops me. I suffer KD so my kids can have a secure childhood.

KD had wanted to go to the US to pursue his MBA and his mother made him promise he would not get back a *gori mem*. That is a great Indian middle-class fear—that the son will marry a white woman, and she will not fit in or take care of the in-laws. The dutiful son that he is, KD agreed to marry the Indian girl his family presented before him.

KD disgusts me. Perhaps his love for sex began when he went abroad. The liberalness in the air and the easier availability of women, with none of the pressure of marriage and commitment must have seemed so tempting. I know him better now, and am pretty sure he must have gone for women of all nationalities except Indian. That way, he could have begged forgiveness when he was done with them—citing parental pressure to marry an Indian girl of their choice. If he got an Indian girl into trouble, there would be hell to pay back in India. Her family would raise a furore, so he must have kept away from them.

Many months into the marriage, I was clearing out KD's stuff one morning, making place for some of my own things, when I chanced upon a shoe box tucked away in the corner of a cupboard seldom used. I opened it and instead of shoes, found letters and photographs. There he was, with an Arab girl in one, with a Latin American one in another. There were pictures at the beach, in a bar, in the pool, with many different women. All the pictures were suggestive. And sexual.

And the letters. Explicit and full of sex talk and sleaze. Of sexual positions and anal sex. Of fantasies.

I remember feeling dizzy. What was going on? I was living a lie. That note from the husband was true. KD indeed sleeps around. Was that the reason he was so skilled in bed? The 'chicken pose', his favored position, was the one that he had mastered after practice on so many women. And I am not the first woman he has oiled, to turn me on, to make the sex hotter, and wetter, as he claims?

Had I been blind? Or had I decided to turn a blind eye?

I called my brother. And he told me to not make an issue out of it. This was in the past and I did not have to worry about what KD did when he was not married to me. Most of the boys who get an opportunity do exactly that. It is a rite of passage. A coming of age. That's what my brother told me, so I shut up and did not mention it to KD.

I had no Plan B anyway.

I tried to not think of these things when KD touched me that night. In my mind I wondered which women he had touched. And how he had made love to them. I wondered if he thought of them when he made love to me. Was that the reason he kept his eyes shut—to fantasize about another woman? Or women?

Later, I consoled myself thinking finally he chose me, not them. So I was better off. I had a higher social and moral ground than those sluts. But a little voice nagged at me incessantly. I was not KD's choice. His mother had selected me. He had not married me for love, but for the sake of his family.

I started going through his things—his phone, his emails, even the mail that came home, addressed to him. I still do. I never thought I could be devious or cunning. I check his coat pockets, his trousers, his briefcase—anything that he carries with him. I even smell his clothes for unfamiliar perfume. When he travels for work—and he travels quite often—I call the hotel number, not his cell, to make sure he is in the room. Sometimes I even ask the hotel operator if Mrs. Kapoor is traveling with him. At parties, I watch him closely to see who he is eyeing. My insecurity disgusts me.

I keep quiet and say none of this to KD. And I smile and respond to him as if all is well between us. As if there is no second, third, or nth person in the bedroom with us.

I remember the day KD met Simran.

KD was looking to sell his business. The previous months were full of meetings with private equity managers, investment bankers and tax consultants. KD had been traveling across the world, meeting global pharmaceutical companies interested in buying out the business. Finally, after heated negotiations, one of the big Swedish pharma companies was going to buy the business. The top executives of the firm were coming down to visit the facilities and sign the agreement. They would make their first stop in Delhi where KD managed to fix a dinner with the finance minister and the minister of industries. The team was put up in luxury suites at Hotel Imperial in Connaught Place. They were taken to the Central Secretariat in Lutyen's Delhi and then onward to Chandni Chowk in Delhi's new pride—the Metro. Chandni Chowk blew their minds, when they experienced it on rickshaws.

In Mumbai, the team was to stay at the newly renovated Taj Mahal Hotel at the Gateway of India. The Taj has always been a popular place for the city's hoi polloi, and the terrorist attacks on that fateful night of November 26, 2008, only added to the symbolism of the magnificent hotel—it became a beacon of hope, and a testimony to the undying spirit and courage of Mumbaikars. The team's Mumbai schedule coincided with the launch of the beautiful book, *The Taj at Apollo Bunder*, by the Tata Group.

KD is an influential person and known to the head honchos of the corporate communications team at Tata Sons too. So he managed to get special invites to the event for the team. And what a night that was. Mumbai's glitterati turned up in full force—there were filmstars, business stalwarts, wealthy businessmen, almost everyone who works to make Mumbai the success it is.

After the book launch, KD's party moved to a private banquet hall in the hotel. KD was the star of the evening. The Indian team was jubilant. KD had won over the Swedish executives. It bode well for the Indian business. There was laughter and amusement all around. I participated in the gentle ribbing and cribbing, all the while noticing how my husband soaked in the praise and the adulation. He had the elegance and grace to not gloat. His ability to demonstrate humility, to praise his subordinates, and carry them forward in the vision he has for his company is admirable. No wonder he is so successful, professionally.

Then KD noticed Simran. She was with Ajit, the owner of Sunshine, the agency that handled the bulk of KD's advertising and creative works. As she walked up to us, I looked at her and mused, 'How does anyone get to be that sexy and pretty at our age?'

A beautiful apparition in aubergine. She was wearing a Paithani sari with a golden brocade blouse. I had always felt aubergine was a difficult color to carry off, but on her it looked divine. The sari draped her with such grace, and her movements were fluid in it. I wear saris on formal occasions but find them such a pain. I still have to put safety pins to keep the pleats and *pallu* in place. I don't manage to use the restroom with grace. And here was Simran, looking ravishing, elegant and sexy. She had happy eyes, a generous mouth, and an incredible aura that made you want to look at her a second time. When she opened her mouth, a low, throaty, amused voice greeted KD. And from the word go, my husband was hooked.

Simran had recently joined as head of creative for Sunshine. The owner of Sunshine, Ajit, is an old pal of mine from school, and he introduced Simran to KD with pride and happiness. Simran looked at me with a lovely smile and shook my hand warmly.

KD forgot Ajit was still standing there and that I was next to him. He had eyes only for Simran. My old companion, jealousy, reared up her ugly head again as I wondered if KD was even listening to what Simran was saying. From where I stood, it seemed to me he only followed the contours of her generous, smiling mouth.

All the while, I kept the smile on my face. While others glanced at me surreptitiously, I pretended not to notice and carried on my conversation with Ajit, who looked apologetic.

I have learnt to not unravel. Not in an obvious way.

I see KD cuddle Rishika. He loves her...the one person I think he truly adores. She has him wrapped around her little finger and he can't deny her anything. I cannot think of anyone else in the family who could deprive him of his beloved Sunday nap and have him drive to the other end of town from Pali Hill on a Sunday afternoon—all because she wanted that little 10-rupee toy from Amarsons in Breach Candy.

Has it ever occurred to KD that someone might cheat on Rishika, much the same way in which he has cheated on me? That her life could also be as miserable as mine? I know he will learn. Men learn humility and pain through their daughters. Through her heartbreak and humiliation he will learn. He will understand betrayal. He will understand mental torture. And I want to see how that will change him.

Did he ever think of Geeta again? After all, he had chatted with her many times over the phone before his mother said no. Did he think of the dreams he shattered when they rejected Geeta? Did he feel remorse?

He feels no remorse now. I watch how he never lets go of his phone. As if Simran might send him a message any moment. Disgust wells up in my throat as I think of his philandering again. It is enough to give me courage.

I walk up to him and ask him for his phone. And see the shifty look come back in his eyes. 'Why do you need my phone?' he asks.

—Because I need to call my brother.

—Where is your phone? I am expecting a call from office in five minutes.

—I forgot to charge it. I will only be a minute.

With reluctance he hands me his cell, and watches as I go into the bedroom with it. I know it will be a minute before he comes in, so I quickly scan WhatsApp and his SMSes to see if Simran has left a message. None. I check the call log. No calls from Simran. I quickly dial my brother, and as I reach the count of 20 in my head, in walks KD, as if on cue. He listens to the conversation, and paces back and forth. Then he tells me to give him the phone and walks out chatting with my brother.

He thinks I am a fool. I know he has deleted all the chats and calls with Simran.

I have seen the change in him since he connected with her. The whole gamut of emotions. The happiness, the joy on his face, the excitement of the initial days. You would think KD was walking on sunshine. He was always beaming, extra indulgent with me, and even less critical of Ranvir. And I can see the stress now. And his need to end the relationship with Simran. He is done. Wooed her, bedded her—there is no mystery anymore. Time to walk away.

Gradually, I learnt to recognize the kind of women he went after. Almost all of them were married. Those are the safest, aren't they? They succumb to temptation, and most have kids so they don't want to rock the boat. The women are terrified of being found out, and that's why, when the chase is over and KD loses interest, he gets out of the mess with ease. Simran does not fit the bill. And she seems to have kicked him out of his comfort zone.

People often say that the wife is the last one to know when the husband is having an extra-marital affair. I can confidently state I knew about Simran almost right away. KD started putting in longer work hours, he went for dinners without telling me who he was dining with. His Facebook updates became more detailed, with lovely pictures that he posted alongside. His phone was never out of reach. In the initial days, before he realized I might be suspicious, he was lax with his phone.

I saw email exchanges with Simran—nothing romantic, but almost a hundred a day, telling her about the mundane things in his life and day. Stuff that he never told me about. Pictures of her. Pictures of him and his family. And, of course, he'd hold me at night and whisper her name in his sleep.

How does one describe betrayal?

The act by which you cheat physically on your spouse? Or the act of an unnatural emotional attachment? Or the fact that the world knows that you are cheating on your wife, and she does not? Or perhaps she does, and whenever she meets your friends, she wonders if they are privy to your little secret. Or when the Mrs. before the surname begins to sound hollow. Or when she begins to feel just a little smaller, just a little ashamed of herself. As if she were lacking in something. In bed, in emotions, in looks. As if her shortcomings were the reason you strayed in your marriage.

If I returned the favor to KD, he would throw me out of the house in the blink of an eye. Double standards.

I am considering what to serve for dessert. Should it be macaroons, profiteroles or an apricot or cherry *clafouti*? A fancy-looking *tulipes* with rasberry sorbet perhaps, with the gorgeous aubergine-colored rasberry sorbet in individual shells? Or should it be the Dark Monk— a chocolate mousse cake with chocolate and rasberry filling?

KD is bothered in his relationship with Simran. More than he usually is. I can see it in him. He paces up and down restlessly. At times he goes off for a late-night post-prandial walk. He wakes up at night and watches TV or plays on his iPad. He is gentler with me and has been making tea for me every morning. He is reaching out a lot more for me at night, to make love to me, to hold me. Men can be so transparent. When he is with any of his women, KD makes love to me as a duty, once a week. And even then it is a 'Wham, Bam, Thank You Ma'am' affair. When he is between women, the pace of his lovemaking is leisurely. I enjoy his lovemaking. Despite the fact that I know he cheats. He is a skilled lover. Though I do wonder sometimes if he makes love to the other women in the same manner as he does to me. Is the chicken pose still his favorite one with the other women? And does he massage them? Does he do it more than twice? How many times can he do it with them? He can be insatiable—I know.

Currently, his Facebook profile picture is a shot of the two of us on our Goa holiday last year. It is a great picture that Ranvir took of us. We were running on the beach, and I surged ahead of KD. In the moment that he caught up with me, and picked me up by my waist, Ranvir took the picture. It has both of us laughing, looking happy.

People can be so unbelievably stupid and naive. Every time I see lovey-dovey spouse posts and pictures on FB, it makes me think there is something wrong in that relationship. Why does one feel the need to post: 'I am blessed to have you (the wife/husband's name) in my life?', or, 'There is no love like ours.' Or even 'Sweetheart'! They are only trying to convince themselves that all is well in their world, and we all should believe it too. And when KD starts posting my pictures all over his phone, his FB page, I know he is sending out a message. To the woman he wants to dump. To me. To himself.

When KD hangs up the phone, I tell him casually, 'I forgot to tell you that Simran was here.'

I watch the color drain from his face. He sputters, 'When?'

'She came by this afternoon. Apparently she had tried to reach you in office, but you were unavailable.'

He tries to compose his face—he looks comical while he affects indifference—and says, 'Why did she come though? What did she say? Did you meet her?'

I pick up a package near me and wave it in front of him. 'No, I was not home when she came by. She left this packet with the maid. She wanted you to have it.'

A multitude of expressions cross my husband's face—fear, horror, anger, distress, relief. He turns a deep red but striving to affect nonchalance, says, 'Did you see what was in it?'

I raise an eyebrow and say, 'I don't know. Maybe some office stuff. You know I don't open your mail.'

KD struggles to control his tremble as he takes the packet and moves towards the study. His shoulders almost sag with relief that I have not been curious, or suspicious, and have not seen the contents of the package.

'Why don't you open it here?' I find myself saying. I am deriving perverse pleasure in his discomfort.

He says, 'Oh it's nothing important. These must be the initial rushes of the post-merger ad campaign. I guess she came here to deliver them because these are confidential. I will be out for dinner my love.'

'Darling,' I say. 'What shall I serve for dessert at the director's party? The *tulipes* with rasberry sorbet, or the Monk?'

KD is distracted. He mumbles, 'Monk should be good.'

He shuts the door to the study after him. I hear him pick up the paper knife and open the envelope gently.

I read somewhere what Sandra Boyden once said about chocolate:

'As with most fine things, chocolate has its season. There is a simple memory aid that you can use to determine whether it is the correct time to order chocolate dishes: any month whose name contains the letter A, E, or U is the proper time for chocolate.'

Monk it shall be. It is April, the cruelest month. I do have a Plan B. I smile.

Veera

I can feel Piya holding my hand. She caresses it softly and tells me she is thinking of running the Mumbai Marathon in six months. 'By that time, Mom, you better wake up. I want you to see me run. Wake up, and if you want to still stay in this room, you can. You will get a lovely view of the sea link where we will begin the race. Else, you had better come to the finish line at VT and see me finish the race. Later we can go for a south Indian breakfast at Matunga. And we will eat a Mysore *masala dosa* and *idlis* and *vadas* dunked in *sambar*. Don't sleep so long Mom. I need you.'

Silently I bless my Piya, my youngest one. She is quiet and shy. Maybe because she saw the conflict between Namita and me, Piya has always been gentle with me. Sometimes I wish she would not be so sacrificing, that she would go out into the world and do things for herself. When I told her I wanted her help in the catering business, she did not even hesitate before offering to work with me. Our clients like her. She is calm, and seldom gets ruffled. While Mana is more creative, Piya is efficient and organized. They both make a great team and have been so successful.

How long has it been since I have been in this vegetable state? I have no idea, though it seems forever. My children are with me now, but I wonder how long it will be before their patience runs out. Before they tire of this constant vigil. Before the medical bills become too high, and they begin to resent my being in a coma. After all, I have outlived my usefulness for my children. They are married, at least KD and Piya are, and they have their own families. Namita has no need for me. Over the years, I have seen a change come over my children. Whereas earlier, the girls would say they were coming to Mom's house, now they say they are coming over to KD's house. Mana is ever loving, but now she runs the kitchen and organizes the household. I felt a twinge in the initial days, then consoled myself saying that is the way of the world. The old has to be replaced by the new, and as *baaji* used to say, everyone worships the rising sun, not the one that is setting.

When I got married, I came into a house that had the bitter smell of failure. A bitterness that I had added to as well. When our alliance was arranged, I was only three years old. I know you young people find it strange now, but at three, the alliance was already too late. In our times, parents tried to fix up a marriage as soon as a girl was born. That way, they were spared the pain of looking for a groom when she was older and one could also get boys from good families. My older sister Nimmi was one when her marriage was arranged with a landowning family near Lahore.

My husband, Gurujitji's family was very wealthy in Rawalpindi. They owned land in Potohar where they grew wheat. Gurujitji was the only son of the oldest brother so he was a prize catch. My family promised them, among other things, 500 acres of our own land near Theha Khalsa. Partition was not even a topic when I was born.

All of us lost everything when we escaped to India after the Partition. Even though my family had sent some money and jewelry ahead, to trustworthy families in Delhi, in the aftermath of the Partition it was simply not enough. We could not even buy a single house that would keep us all together. Forget the house, we were all at the mercy of the generous families who housed us till we managed to find our feet in that new land. And the whole family that had lived together in the Rawalpindi *haveli* never lived together in our new homeland.

I was married off in 1954, when was only 13. I missed Nimmi. I missed Rawalpindi and our whole family, but I had begun to enjoy school and made friends. When I got my monthly periods that *beyji* called 'Aunty who visits every month', I was told that I was ready for marriage. *Beyji* explained to me that I could have babies now, and it was time for me to go to my husband's house. Gurujitji was 18 at the time, handsome, six feet tall, fair, with hazel-colored eyes and pink lips. He had a certain sophistication about him.

Even before I could have a loving husband, I had lost him. Gurujitji was cool and distant. He did not hit me or drink or have any vices. But there was nothing he wanted to share with me, no laughter and no happiness. For many years, I never saw a smile on his face, never heard him laugh out loud at a joke. He was preoccupied with the business of survival.

I was too young to bear any grudges. Gurujitji was the only breadwinner in that whole family and the burden of that responsibility was almost too much to bear. The family had fled to Mumbai, where they had no other relatives or friends, and from what my mother-in-law, *maaji*, lamented, I figured they had a very bad time. They had to stay in the camp at Kolwada, where they got food barely fit for dogs. There were only a dozen taps for the camp with thousands of refugees, and there was no electricity. Gurujitji was only 13 years old at the time, and he had to step in to support the family. He never told me, but apparently he worked as a hawker on the streets selling trinkets and was beaten up by the street gangs that were fiercely territorial. He worked on the docks loading and unloading materials. By the time I was brought to Mumbai, Gurujitji and his family of three sisters and *maaji* stayed in a one-bedroom flat on Chimbai Lane in Bandra. He was personal secretary to one of the builders in Mumbai and he worked long hours. But *sethji* was a decent person and generous with us.

Instead of all the dowry and riches they were promised, my in-laws only got a measly few gold ornaments. They were in no position to say no to the alliance. They were no longer rich *zamindars* and it was not possible to get a wealthy match for their son in that environment. Who in their right mind would agree to marry their daughter into a poor family that had the additional burden of marrying off three unwed daughters? My family also had no option. They could not pay a dowry for me anymore. They were grateful that Gurujitji's family kept their promise; else I would have been shamefully unmarried for the rest of my life.

In my marital home, there was the burden to run the household, burden to marry off the girls, burden to support other family members. In those post-Partition days, families and relatives came pouring in from the other side of the line, and you could not turn anyone away. In those days, some refugees, as we were called, moved many times in search for work or a better life. Those years, I only remember cooking and cleaning. I was only 13. But no one thought of that. Only 13, ravaged by the Partition, but no one knew that. Gurujitji had been destroyed as well. He had grown up in a wealthy environment and as the oldest son, had been pampered and trained for his rightful position as the head of the family. After 1947, though, while the privilege of being the head of the family remained, all else was lost. There was no land, no money, no servants, no pride. What he inherited instead was a bagful of discontent, unhappiness, disenchantment, bitterness and anger. For a young boy of 18, it must have seemed so overwhelming. Perhaps that was the reason he lost his youthfulness and the happiness that comes with it.

1947. I was six that year, in Rawalpindi, and too young to know what was wrong. There was excitement in the air. We would eavesdrop on conversations between the adults who discussed Partition. India would get divided—one country for the Muslims and one for the Hindus. No one thought that the Sikhs needed a homeland. Or, for that matter, the Sindhis.

In the last few months before the fighting broke out, we started sleeping on the terrace of the house. The nights were hot and muggy but the terrace was full of fascinating things. The men had been working hard and had installed big brick stoves. On one, there was a cauldron of hot water and on another, hot oil. There were bottles of acid lined up against the wall and we were forbidden to peep from the terrace. All the men of the house were on duty on rotation. They had to guard the perimeter of the property and also the terrace where we all slept.

All night, we would hear drunk men stand under our door, and scream, 'Oh *sardarji*. Wait till we come for your lovely daughters. And take off their clothes and fuck them in front of you. And we will keep them as our whores.'

Sikhs are known for their fierce warrior personas. *Bauji* and his brothers would fume with anger and my brothers would be ready to go kill those wretched drunks. But they would all restrain themselves; they did not want to be provoked into a fight. They were helpless in their anger.

Veerji had joined the Indian army the previous year, when he turned 18. It was his dream job. Ever since he was a little boy, Veerji wanted to wear the soldier's uniform. He was the *chamcha* of all the older boys in the neighborhood who had joined the army and used to come home for the holidays. Veerji hung on to every word they said—where they stayed, their daily routines, their special diets, and the discipline. Most of all, he loved to hear how their regiments had fought in the various wars for the British.

Years later, it used to distress me when my children told me that India had not participated in the World Wars, because we were so far away from Europe. It was beyond their understanding that Indians had belonged to the British army while they ruled over us. And that Indians went where their British *sahibs* told them to go.

Indians fought in the World War I against the Axis forces, where innumerable soldiers were martyred. They died in the battlefield because of the cold weather that they were unprepared for and equipment that they were not familiar with. I remember Jagat *Chacha* whose damaged feet were a big draw with us children. He had fought in World War I, where soldiers had spent most of their time in the trenches. His feet, he said, were never warm and dry. And then he realized that they had turned red and started to smell bad. Before the war was over, the army doctors had cut off the toes on his right foot because they were afraid the infection would spread to the rest of his body. Jagat *Chacha* hobbled painfully, but to young boys like Veerji, that toeless foot was heroic. It represented to them the glory of fighting for one's country and protecting their families and loved ones.

When Veerji got accepted into the 1st Patiala Regiment in the British Army, it was a day of much rejoicing in our family. *Beyji* made *karha parshad*, with dollops of extra sugar and ghee to be distributed after the *ardas* in the gurudwara. That day, the whole family was dressed in its finest and also did the *langar sewa* at the gurudwara. How handsome Veerji looked in his new uniform as he served the *langar* with such happiness. I bet there were many young girls that day who eyed him shyly and wanted to talk to him. That day he still had wisps of hair for a beard. Years later, Veerji would have the lush beard he always wanted, and in my eyes, my already-handsome Veerji looked even more distinguished.

Veerji stayed in the barracks. One night he came home and told us to get ready as soon as possible. He had found a convoy leaving for Amritsar that had space for us. This was too sudden. Even though every evening the elders had been discussing the possibility of leaving for Delhi, no one had planned for the eventuality. In their hearts, no one wanted to leave this house, this land, where we had lived for generations. This house had seen happiness—childbirths, marriages, festivals. For decades the house had reverberated with the sounds of growing children and their mothers; of grandparents who had retired from active life and enjoyed their grandchildren and presided over family occasions. It had seen sad moments too—little children who died in wombs, mothers who died in childbirth, and grandparents who passed away. It had seen its share of fights, between the women of the household, between its sons, but it was a source of pride for the family that it had never broken up. That we still stood together as one.

The convoy was to leave early in the morning. The elders locked themselves up in a room and there were furious, hushed exchanges in the room. We climbed up to the ventilators above the doorway to eavesdrop. All we heard were fragments of their conversation like 'massacre', 'bloodbath', 'rape', 'leave it like this', 'no time', 'jewelry'. I came to know later that some elders had wanted to stay on in Rawalpindi, but Veerji had pleaded with them. He had heard rumors that Rawalpindi would most certainly go to the new Muslim nation. There would be a bloodbath, or, at the very least, mass looting and rapes. Had we all not heard the belligerent tones of the drunk men under our house?

Finally my grandfather prevailed, and the family decided to leave Rawalpindi with the convoy.

I sometimes wonder now what would have happened if the British had announced the partition lines of India and Pakistan in the Punjab before August 15, 1947. Would the violence have been on such a large scale? Would so many people have been murdered, so many wounded and maimed, so many women and girls raped? Would there have been so many unclaimed women and bastard children? *Beyji* believed that the bloodbath was inevitable and in the final analysis, the date for announcing the boundaries became insignificant. For months tension had been brewing, and insignificant events had blown up into fights and scuffles. A dead pig thrown in front of the mosque, a Hindu woman eve-teased by Muslim boys, groceries being refused to a Muslim family from the local Hindu store they had frequented all their lives—all these became reasons to distrust each other. The hurt, confusion, anger and bitterness had to find an outlet. There was no stopping the pent up emotions of millions of people who got displaced. Suddenly, the only homes they had ever known were no longer safe to live in and the very neighbors they had grown up with were out to rape their daughters, kill their sons, and loot their homes. There had to be a flare-up. And more than 15 million people were caught up in the transfer in Punjab alone. Can you imagine? There are millions of stories, millions of unsung heroes, and millions of normal, decent human beings who became savages for that period of time. And no matter what any community claims, all of us—Indians and Pakistanis—were equally brutal.

Beyji was very distraught. There was no time to get Nimmi from her in-laws' house. *Bauji* had gone to Nimmi's house the previous week and asked her in-laws to send Nimmi home with him. They had refused. They did not even consider the possibility of relocating across the Wagah border for a few months till the violence died down.

There was no time to say goodbye. I did not understand then that I would never come back to that house. To the only home where I had truly been happy.

Looking back I wish I had understood. Or at least got time to say goodbye to some of the things I loved dearly in that house. Like the old mango trees that we climbed to get *kairi* and mangoes. To the guava tree which was my refuge when I needed to hide if *beyji* was angry and wanted to hit me, or when I did not want to share my sweetmeats with anyone. To the *henna* tree whose leaves we would pluck and grind on the *sil-batta* before applying on our hands. To the *ber* tree, whose small red tart fruit we all fought for. To the platform on the banyan tree outside, where we spent many lazy afternoons pretending to study. To the swings on the tree where we took turns, to see who went the highest.

There was no time to call the Muslim *dhobi's* daughter who was my constant companion and would not come to India. I would have kissed the Guru Granth Sahib in the house one last time, touched the walls, floor, every part of the house once more so I would remember it on my fingers forever.

And my dear sister Nimmi. I did not get to hug and kiss her. Nimmi who was only 12 that year. Who was brutally raped in front of her nine-month-old son, her husband and father-in-law. Again and again, while my little nephew cried pitiably to see his mother in that state. Nimmi, who was such a firebrand and would fight tooth and nail even for a piece of *revadi*. Whose son was thrown against the wall to silence him. Whose family was killed in so cold-blooded a manner, whose house was taken over by the local landlord. I never got to say bye to her.

India got its independence. I lost my home. And my freedom.

We left in the dark of the night. *Beyji* made us wear two (or was it three?) layers of clothing. We also wore extra underwear that had some jewelry stitched in its lining. Finally, all of us were given a small bottle of rat poison. *Beyji* kissed me and said, 'You will be with me always. But if I get lost, or you can't find any one of us, eat this. Don't go with anyone else.'

I was horrified that my own mother would give me poison and ask me to eat it, but I knew better than to throw a tantrum at that point. We were all cooped up in the back of a truck. I felt very sad seeing my proud grandparents crouching like servants in that truck. It was a long journey, with frequent stops along the way. We could hear noises outside, but were told to not peep out. We had no idea how long we were in the truck. You know, I always think of that time when I smell *aloo paranthas*. The ladies had made those for the journey. And we ate lots of them through the journey. Then again, had I known these were the last ones from my Rawalpindi home, I would have savored each bite, instead of eating them mindlessly. Even today, *aloo paranthas* are my go-to food when I am feeling sad. They bring me closer to the people I loved.

My first glimpse of India was when we crossed the Wagah border. To me it looked no different from Rawalpindi. The people looked the same too. Our first stop was at Amritsar where we stayed in a *dharamsala* near the Golden Temple. For a week, while we children played merry in the large compound of the gurudwara, standing in line for the simple *langar* of *dal* and *roti*, the elders deliberated on the next course of action. My *chacha* wanted to go to Allahabad because his wife had some family there and he could join their business. Veerji wanted us to come to Delhi since he was posted there. My older *tayaji* decided to go to Mumbai because his Sindhi friends had moved there and told him there was plenty work in trading there. And the younger *tayaji* decided to stay on in Amritsar, hoping that when things settled down, he could go back to Rawalpindi and get started. My grandparents also decided to stay on in Amritsar. The rest of the family would join them back in Rawalpindi when the tensions eased off.

My family was never together again. No one ever got to go back to that beloved Rawalpindi *haveli* again.

Did we have a bad time? Yes we did. It is distressing to lose one's homeland, to be uprooted from all that one has known all one's life. It is difficult to get used to the idea that no one knows you in the new country. Yet, when I compare my experience to that of so many others, I think we were blessed. Yes, we were broke and poor, and at the mercy of generous families in India. My family went to live in the outhouse of one of *beyji's* distant cousins. It was a one-bedroom house. While Veerji went back to join the army and hustled for an apartment for all of us, *bauji* went out looking for work. He managed to find a job as an accountant for a Marwari whose Muslim accountant had left for Pakistan. Mother cleaned and cooked in the family's home.

Every day, for months, *bauji* went to the various refugee camps around Delhi to look for Nimmi. He submitted details about her family and her. There was no information on her for three months. Then *bauji* met someone from Rawalpindi who told him what had become of Nimmi.

I admire Punjabis and Sikhs for their valor and enterprise. Which other community has suffered so much and yet re-started their lives from scratch when they moved to India? We are brave, but after that day, the light went out of my parents' eyes. They looked decades older and became sad people. They blamed themselves for letting Nimmi die. *Beyji* never quite slept well after that. They both worked hard so that the body and mind would be able to forget.

Delhi felt alien, and I was awed by it. Lutyen's Delhi was neat, clean, and so green. In those days there were *tongas* everywhere. I loved to sit on these horse carriages and see the new city unravel before my eyes. I walked all the way from India Gate to the Viceroy's residence, that later became the Rashtrapati Bhavan. Veerji also took us to Connaught Circus one evening. I thought there was no city prettier than Delhi. I even saw Nehru one day. He was in his open car that crossed us in Connaught Circus. He looked at us on the roadside and waved out to me. In those days, the politicians were not scared of the people they were leading. They did not have scores of police men cordoning them off from the *janta*. We all loved Nehru.

I heard horror stories everywhere. Of women being raped in front of their family members. Of their breasts and genitals being cut off. Of them being forced to marry Muslim men. Of tattoos imprinted on their private parts. Of women coming to India and being rejected by their families because they had been raped and were spoilt goods. I would feel breathless imagining what had happened to Nimmi, my brave, firebrand sister no one could win an argument against. I used to get nightmares thinking about Nimmi naked in front of strange men. She was so shy at home. I was careless about undressing in front of *beyji*, Nimmi, and my girl cousins, but Nimmi would always change behind the curtain in our room. She would never let me take a bath with her either. What shame my Nimmi must have felt!

In the years gone by, I have often woken up in a cold sweat when I dream of Nimmi. The cruelty of being raped in front of her husband and his family. Their shame at not being able to protect her. I often wonder when the fight must have gone out of Nimmi. It must have been when she saw her infant child being murdered. Which mother can survive that?

I always thank Waheguru that I did not have a bad time and I was spared that horror. So what if the gentleman in that Delhi house took me into a special little room whenever he could. And would make me touch him and take his manhood in my mouth. He would keep stroking my hair and clutch it tight just before he made guttural sounds and something wet and sticky filled my mouth.

He would caress my breasts and touch me down there. He would insert his finger and also tried to insert his manhood in me. All the while, he would plant small kisses on my whole body and tell me I was his special girl. That he was only trying to give me love because I had lost so much. He wanted me and my parents to be happy and safe. This was our little secret he said. In turn, he would give me candy or sometimes money. I would keep the money quietly in *beyji's* cupboard. She always thought it was Veerji who left money for her. It was my small contribution. I always scrubbed my body after he had touched it, and some days, I couldn't walk, because I was so sore in that place. But like I said, it was nothing compared to what others were going through.

Within a year, Veerji managed to get an army quarters, and we moved there. Slowly life limped back to as normal as it could. I started school. I finally had new clothes—two sets of them. Every evening *beyji* would wash one set so I could wear fresh clothes the next day. *Beyji* filled that little house with her love. And cooking. The smells of *rajma*, *chhole*, and *saag* made that house feel like home.

I had only begun to settle into my new life, feeling happy at last, when they carried out the marriage ceremony that brought me to Gurujitji and his family in Mumbai. Or Bombay as I knew it then. I had not wanted to leave *beyji*, but I could not question them.

When I got married, I shivered at the thought of being touched. But he never noticed. How could he? In that one-bedroom apartment that reeked of anger against me for not getting the promised dowry, he would touch me only at night when the urge took over. I had to be quiet. I had to stifle my pain when he would come on top of me and move with almost savage intensity. I learnt to let my mind wander—to Rawalpindi, to my gauva tree—till he was done. And when he would shudder and roll off me, I would quietly get up and go to the bathroom to clean up. Gurujitji would be snoring by the time I got back.

When I see KD hugging Mana, I like it. I wish them happiness and love and laughter. And I hope he indulges her a lot. When I was much younger, I used to make it a point to buy an expensive sari or a piece of jewelry for Mana. And giftwrap it and give it to KD to give it to my lovely daughter-in-law. I wish I had known how it felt—to have a husband who cared, a husband who indulged, a husband who would have loved me. I had not wanted much. A smile from Gurujitji when I made the dishes he was fond of or when I opened the door for him in the evening. I craved for a touch on my shoulder, or my arm, that would tell me he cared. Some conversation that would tell me he cared enough to share his life with me. That he loved me. I would not have felt so alone, so unloved, so unwanted then. Maybe my heart would not have shriveled up so much that when, years later, he became attached to me, I had nothing to give him—except for the food I served, the shirts I laundered, the house that I kept meticulously clean, and the children I bore him.

Namita

To: namitap@gmail.com
From: Piyar@gmail.com
Jun 23, 2013
12.30 p.m.

I am sitting in the visitors lobby at Lilavati right now. I needed to get out of that room. KD is there right now. Seeing Mom lying lifeless on that bed is too much to bear. She is hooked up to all kinds of machines. Sometimes I tell myself she is only in a deep sleep and she deserves the rest. Really, Namita, if you could see her right now, she looks peaceful, more peaceful than she has ever been. Ever since I remember her, Mom was always on her toes, always busy.

The Lilavati lobby is such a depressing place—loads of people keeping a vigil for their loved ones. Some are reading, others are praying silently. Many more are just sitting around chatting with their relatives or friends, or even commiserating with other people. There is also a multi-faith room where people go to pray. And of course, there is food everywhere! How much we Indians love eating! The café on the first floor has decent tea and coffee and a range of snacks. On occasion, it feels like party time here!

I marvel at the number of lives Mom has touched. Apart from family and friends, she has women from her *satsang*, people she met at the gurudwara, even her long-term clients who come to commiserate. The tiny, spritely thing really has created a whole world around her!

Death seems like a long way off for now, but I have plans for my 45th birthday. I will write a note and email/snail mail it to all the people I want to reach out to, who have impacted my life. I will tell them exactly what I feel about them! How does that sound?

It occurs to me, though, that in India we are lucky. Sure, family can be a problem because we don't know how to mind our business, but it is also our backbone. It supports us when we are down and you need not ever be alone. Anand's friend, Dr. Chahal, has just moved from London and is with the Tata Memorial Hospital. She came to visit us at Lilavati and commented on how in London, cancer patients come alone for their chemotherapy sessions. In contrast, in India, patients are accompanied by at least two family members on every visit. Anand told her that was unthinkable here—no family member would ever leave you alone!!

I felt so bad reading your email. I know you carry this anger, Namita. And I ask myself, can we really see the same person in such different ways?

Mom is partial to KD, but then don't all Indian mothers have that for their sons? Look at Anand's mother. She fawns over him like he were a kid still. When we visit them she makes all his favorite things, not Nikki's. Not even after Meera passed away and Nikki needed so much love and support. Perhaps it has to do with the fact that most of them had such unhappy marriages and they lean heavily on their sons. We know Mom did. That silly granny of ours made her life miserable. I think Dad loved her in his own way, but he just did not express it in time. By the time his need for her increased, Mom had already found an outlet for her happiness. She always thanked Dad for it, but she had moved on from him. I don't really blame her.

And I know you feel she did not love you Namita, but she did. She is so proud of you—every single photo you have ever taken has been carefully filed away and she is always showing it off to the children and her friends. She always felt that you were this bright, sparkly thing who would find her groove in the world. She expected too much of you I think. And she bore you down with her expectations. But that was her love for you Nams.

To: Piyar@gmail.com
From: namitap@gmail.com
Jun 24, 2013
10.15 p.m.

Is mom doing any better? Any more reports?

LOL on your 45th birthday idea. Somehow I know at least one person who is getting that letter from you. Let me read that letter please, and I bet that person is going to have a hard time!

Mom loved me you say? And expected great things from me? And is proud of me? When she was so derogatory about what I wanted in life?

I wanted to be a photographer and she thought it was a useless pursuit. In her opinion, all 'fast' girls wanted to get into the film or TV business. She told me I had no talent, that men would use me for my looks and then dump me when they were all done with me. Man, the woman must have secretly gloated when I broke up with my boyfriends.

Instead, Mom forced me to take science in junior college because she wanted me to become a doctor. And not any kind of doctor. She wanted me to be a dentist, because it meant that I would find a good husband, have decent working hours, and also manage my house and kids. There was no question on whether I wanted to be a doctor, forget being a dentist. Of course I never intended to be a doctor, so I did not study that hard.

Marriage, marriage! As if a husband was the only thing that would define me. Only popping babies would give me the role of my life, and only motherhood would complete me.

Do you remember in college, when that agency head from Nobuka came scouting for talent? Abhishek Mathur? I applied on a whim. I was surprised when he even considered me because I had no experience. The only pictures I had ever taken were from the black-and-white camera Sangs had lent me. He said I had potential and he would test out to see what I could come up with.

That year was so great for me Piya. I would get up every morning, excited beyond reason. And the first thing that came to my mind was, 'I am so glad to be alive'. For once in my life it stopped bothering me that Mom did not fuss over me. I was secretly glad—it meant her focus was on you and KD and she didn't care what I did. It didn't bother me that she would not give me breakfast, or a tiffin, or even kiss me bye. It did not matter that she was so scary that I could not share the excitement of my day with her. Each day would be different. Sometimes, I would assist a seasoned photographer on a shoot all over town. On other days, I would be given a camera and told to go scout for locations and take pictures. Or I would be asked to sit in on a discussion for a commercial to be shot. I learnt, and absorbed, and there was nothing I would not do to keep this going.

From my first salary, a princely sum of ₹2,000, I bought a little something for all of you. A pair of cheap earrings for you because you always stole mine, t-shirts for KD and Dad, and a nightgown for Mom. I gave these to KD because he was the only one who knew about my internship. And we both decided that we would tell Mom about my job then. Oh how she fussed over KD!

Hugging and kissing him because she thought he was the one who had bought her the gifts. 'My darling son, the only one who cares so much about us. God bless you. I wish Namita was also like you, instead of the sulky child she is. Maybe you will learn from your brother Namita.'

KD was embarrassed and began to speak. I signaled to him to say nothing. Suddenly, the gifts, the excitement, had lost their meaning for me. Mom could keep thinking he had bought the nightgown for her. It seems like a small thing to hold a grudge against, but that day, I really hurt. And I think it was the beginning of my disengagement with her. Her sarcastic tone still grates on my nerves. Mom wore that nightgown for years, until the pink flowers on it had faded into nothingness. After some time, I derived vicious pleasure from it. Little did she know that the nightgown had come from me, not from her darling KD. From the Namita she loved to criticize. From the Namita whose photography she always hated. Served her right.

To: namitap@gmail.com
From: Piyar@gmail.com
Jun 25, 2013
11 a.m.

Sweetie,

You never told me in all these years that those earrings were a gift from you. I loved them. And wore them all through college. You won't believe it, but last year when I was cleaning out my stuff, I found them. That day Meera was over, and she liked them so much I gave them to her. Nikki returned them to me last month and now Garima has them and wears them all the time. What memories, and what amazing value for money sis!!! Thank you. Love you...

KD and you should have told her. What makes you think she would not have been happy Namita? You know, when you started college, you actually wore a sulky expression all the time.

I used to be scared of you. You would snap at me if I took any of your clothes. (Well I still did, I just got smarter at hiding the fact!)

You refused to share anything with me. Thank God I had Ayesha with me.

You would sit on your bed with a scowl on your face, and a book in your hands, all those years.

Mom at least had the courage to tell you that you were a sulky thing. The rest of us just made ourselves scarce.

Mom is proud of you Namita. All of us are. The great Namita Kapoor—the only one to have won so many awards in our family. KD is a little behind you! And I haven't even begun!! LOL

And ya, that letter will be the worst of all. I can forgive everyone in my life, except for that bastard.

Nikki

Nikki entered Meera's room. It was in perfect condition, just the way 'fussy' Meera liked it. She loved to read. Each of Meera's books had to be dusted and kept back just the way she liked them. Her books had to be organized in a particular way, and that changed every month. Some months, the books were organized according to authors. In other months, they were arranged according to genre, or whatever else took Meera's fancy. Once Meera had the brainwave of color coordinating them. So the reds were in one place, the browns in another. She didn't like that too much because there was no balance and she told Nikki, 'Why can't they make covers in different colors? Like yellow, or purple, or even gray? Books can look so monotonous in shades of black, white, red and blue.'

Meera's trinkets were kept in an organized chaos on the chest of drawers. Nikki never quite figured out the method in her madness, but Meera seemed to know exactly what was in each pouch or box and pulled them out with ease.

Nikki lay down on Meera's bed. This week it had her favorite purple bedspread with peacocks on it. From this position of repose she viewed Meera's room, though every inch of it was committed to her memory. The purple wall—or was it lavender, or lilac? Nikki had forgotten—was also Meera's choice. She had been all of 11 years old then and wanted to redecorate her room. Nikki remembered with a twist in her heart how the little doll went everywhere with her. She first selected the wallpaper, and then matched her bed linen with it. They both had an argument over the carpet. Nikki was not in favor of buying a carpet for 20 grand, but Meera wheedled and whined till a harassed Nikki gave in.

On her window sill, Meera had placed in a pot the agave plant that she had picked up from their school trip to Jamnagar to see the huge petroleum refinery. She was tickled that marijuana was extracted from this plant, and had wanted to try it at home too.

The walls were full of pictures—Meera's first day at school, a collage of her early years, the many holiday pictures with Nikki, Anil, and Jai, and with friends.

Nikki closed her eyes for a moment. And in that moment, Meera was back to being the three-hour-old infant who was brought to her from the nursery for her feed. Nikki remembered looking down at her and being fascinated. *Was this what was growing in my body all this while? Feeding off me?* She was in awe. With her finger she traced the baby's face—her closed eyes, her cheeks, her lips. And the baby's mouth instinctively moved towards the finger, seeking warmth, seeking milk.

Nikki remembered the first time Meera opened her eyes. She was holding her, looking at her face, when suddenly the baby opened her eyes. Later, Nikki read that newborns don't see very well, and she must have looked hazy and unfocused to the baby. But at that moment, Nikki saw herself drowning in love. Meera's eyes reflected complete acceptance of who she was.

How can you describe a love that takes you utterly by surprise? One that makes you want to protect the person with all your life. But I failed her. I did not manage to protect my baby, and I loved her more than life itself.

When Meera was in the hospital, Nikki sat by her bedside, night and day. By then, everyone was resigned to the fact that Meera would not survive. Those drips that fed her medicines and food had caused too much pain. The tube under her nose that gave her oxygen seemed to Nikki like a noose. In those moments, Nikki wanted Meera to give up the fight. She would hold Meera's hand, rub it gently, and think, *Let go, baby. Don't fight the pain anymore. Go to a peaceful place.*

When Meera was young and would get hurt, Nikki would quickly gather her in her arms and kiss the place where she had hurt herself. And then she would say, 'There, see, mama has made the hurt go away.' And Meera would smile through her tears, and hug Nikki and give her a big sloppy kiss.

How I wish my kisses did indeed possess magical powers that would have healed my baby, eased her pain, and made her well again? But I failed her.

Nikki's eyes welled up with tears and she snuggled her face into Meera's pillow. She couldn't smell Meera anymore. That smell that she loved so much. At night when Meera would sleep, Nikki would creep into her bed, cuddle her, and take in her smell. When Meera was an infant, she had that clean baby smell. Then came the powdery smell of Johnson's baby powder. Later, when Meera grew up, sometimes it was the smell of young sweat, or the deodorant that Meera had learnt to use. To Nikki these were all wonderful smells, the smell of her baby, and she would drink them all in. She missed the warm body next to her.

Almost a year ago, when Meera came back from school and started complaining of a headache, Nikki paid little attention in the beginning. There were a number of reasons that her head could be hurting. Maybe Meera was sleep-deprived. There was so much work in school. Maybe her eyesight had become weaker.

Maybe she had gotten into a fight with her friends and this was a psychosomatic pain. Or she had not been eating a proper breakfast and hunger was giving her a headache. Nikki took Meera for an eye check-up, gave her paracetamol, and chatted with her about her friends to try and figure what was wrong. Then on a number of occasions Meera threw up, and she started getting fatigued faster. Nikki thought it might be her periods that were causing the problem.

One evening at dinner, Meera fainted. And Nikki and Anil panicked. They rushed Meera to the nearby Ambani hospital where the doctor ordered a battery of tests. When Dr. K called them for a consultation, Anil had an important meeting and could not make it. For Nikki it was the longest afternoon in her life. She sat there, in front of a panel of doctors, barely able to understand what was being said to her. It was as if she was under a waterfall, and the voices were coming from somewhere beyond—muted and garbled. Cancer. A malignant tumor in the brain. This could not be happening to them. To their Meera. All Nikki remembers of that afternoon is calling Anil. Anil would not take the call because he was in his meeting. But she had stopped thinking. She pressed the redial button again, and again, and yet again. Anil finally picked up the phone and whispered, 'What is it? I am busy.' In a dull voice she said, 'You need to come here. Now.'

Nikki sat stone-faced as the doctors spoke incoherently around her. Her tongue felt heavy like lead and her brain was unable to form intelligible words. Someone had gotten her a cup of coffee and she sat, holding it in her hand. In her mind, she was thinking that she needed to get out of the place. Meera and Jai would be waiting at home for her. They must be back from school. She had promised to make them penne in white sauce for their evening snack. The maid did not know how to do it well enough. She had to take Meera to buy her a new dress for the school party. The girl did not want to repeat any clothes. She wanted a new dress for every single party, and since all her friends were turning 16 around the same time, there were so many clothes to be bought.

When Anil walked into the doctor's chambers, Nikki felt like she was about to collapse. He walked up to her, and when he held her hand, all strength left her body. She leaned on him and said, 'Can you believe it? Our baby is dying.' And her tears broke through. Nikki never knew she had so many tears in her. They wouldn't stop. They didn't stop when the doctors detailed what was happening. They refused to stop when Anil led her out of the room. They poured all the way home. For a very long time, Nikki and Anil sat in the car in the parking lot, lost in thought. They did not know how to face the children at home.

How do you tell your child, who is a month short of her 16th birthday, that she has a tumor, so far gone that she may not live till her next birthday?

Meera was terribly excited about her birthday. On his last trip to the US, Anil had picked up a short lace dress in onion pink for her. Meera loved it, and had spent the next few weekends buying shoes and accessories to go with it. She wanted to curl her gorgeous long hair and wear make-up too. Nikki did not approve. These school years were not for make-up and hairdos. She had to study hard and get admission into a good college. But Meera was totally involved in clothes, make-up, and her cell phone. Before every party, mother and daughter would get into a fight, because Nikki could not figure why clothes could not be repeated for parties. It was not as if she was buying cheap clothes from roadside shops on Hill Road or Linking Road. Each dress had a fancy label, and it was expensive. When Nikki would tell her, 'We did not grow up like this. I had four dresses and wore them to all occasions. Not like you, with no regard for money,' Meera would roll her eyes and retort, 'That was your problem Mom. Things have changed. Just because you don't like dressing up does not mean that I shouldn't either.' Nikki would suppress the urge to slap her.

The clubhouse in their building had been booked for the dance party and a DJ had been shortlisted. Meera wanted only pizzas for dinner and loads of soft drinks. She also did not want parents on the prowl, but Anil told her they would check in every half hour. Nikki had also organized for the photographer to come with some props—large hats, funky scarves, and glasses so kids could get their pictures taken.

What for? Nikki thought now. The normal way of the world is that life comes full circle. You are born, you grow up, you have kids, you die. Why was my cycle disturbed? Why should a parent have to set fire to the child's cremation pyre? Why should a parent have to hold her child's hand and watch helplessly as life seeps away from her? Why should Meera's life have been cut short?

There was so much Meera had wanted to do, that Nikki and Anil had wanted to do with Meera and Jai. Holidays were a time for family bonding. Every year, they let the children decide the holiday they wanted to take. The kids would spend endless weeks scouting out holiday destinations. Then they would make a presentation to the parents—on where they wanted to go and what they wanted to see. Dinners were full of discussion and fun. Jai wanted pure adventure—Antarctica, Peru, the Amazon rainforest—and Meera wanted all that as well as shopping. Anil and Nikki loved to spend time separately with the kids, and at their most vulnerable, the kids would share everything with the parents.

Now, Jai had lost his smile. And his voice. The silence in the house was claustrophobic, whereas it used to reverberate with the incessant noise of the kids earlier. They were constantly fighting with each other. There was nothing they could agree on—what program to watch, what food to eat, where to sit and study. Meera would not let Jai enter her room, or he would take her socks, or she would eat his share of candy and they were always arguing. Now, the candy sat untouched in the fridge, Jai would not watch TV; he would just quietly read in his room. Nikki's heart hurt at Jai's pain. He had been so brave in Meera's last days. He did not complain about the neglect he went through; he sat next to Meera when he got back and would tell her stories about school. When her nausea got too much, Jai would rub her back gently and talk to her in a soothing voice.

I have lost one child and the other one has lost his childhood.
What can be worse for a parent than to see her child suffer? When you bring a child into this world, you are responsible for them. You want to protect them from everything. Where did I go wrong? Was I a negligent mom? If I had heeded Meera's headache early on, could we have saved her? Perhaps her tumor would not have grown so much. What other signs did I miss?

Nikki had lost her sleep after Meera's birth. She would wake up at night, put her hand on Meera's little chest to make sure she was still breathing. She would put her finger under her nose to check.

Surgery was ruled out for Meera's tumor because it was huge and could be potentially fatal. Chemotherapy was the only recourse, though the doctors were not very optimistic about that either.

Nikki and Anil did not have a plan. They did not know what they would tell Meera. When they walked into the house, the intuitive child that Meera was, she knew something was terribly wrong. Nikki's face was ashen and Anil seemed broken. Nikki tried being brave, when every part of her heart was splintered into a million pieces and her mind could not form a single coherent thought.

How do you tell your child that she is going to die? That she will not join her friends in sharing secrets and giggle at stupid things. That she will not know the joy of falling in love, of a first kiss. That she will not know the pleasure and pain of studying and getting her dream job? That she will not be able to buy the Mini Cooper she wanted when she grew up. That she will never get her driving license. That she won't know the happiness of finding the right life partner. That she won't wear mehndi or have the big, fat Indian wedding. That she will not experience childbirth and the pure joy kids bring to you. That she won't be around for Jai's kids to call her bua.

Nikki struggled to keep her tears at bay as Meera came up to hug her. Anil sat down heavily on the sofa and looked down. Meera looked at Nikki and said, 'What's wrong? Mom you can tell me. I am not a kid. I can tell something is wrong.'

Anil spoke. He, who could never bear to ever see Meera in pain, was the one to break the news to her. When Meera was a baby, and had to get her shots, Anil would hover outside the doctor's chamber because he was too soft-hearted to hold her at that time. As soon as the shots were done, he would rush into the doctor's chamber, scoop Meera up, mumble sweet nothings in her ears, kiss her, and console the wailing infant.

He told Meera, 'Sweetheart. The doctors say you have a tumor in your brain.'

Meera looked at them in horror. 'I have cancer?'

—No, no...it's a tumor, and they are going to do their best to cure you. They plan on starting a course of medication first.

—Meds for what?

—To reduce the size of the tumor. And then they will try and operate on it.

Meera turned to Nikki, 'Swear on me, Mom. Tell me the truth.'

The tough thing about motherhood is the fact that you learn to lie. Small little lies to console the baby, like kissing away the pain. Small untruths to discipline them like, I was a straight-A kid in school. I did not have a boyfriend. I never gossip. I never stole money from my parents' wallets. We siblings never fought in front of our parents.

You cover up the paucity of money because you want to give them a good life. You learn to fight behind closed doors because you don't want their tender minds to get upset. Parents can be the biggest liars, manipulators, deceivers, but with the pure intention of protecting their children.

At this moment, when Nikki should have lied, her eyes and face gave her away. In the depth of her anguish, she turned to Anil, 'Don't treat her like a baby. Tell her the truth...she has to learn to handle it.' She turned to Meera and said harshly, 'Dad is lying. Your tumor is malignant, Meera.'

The world swam before Nikki's eyes and she fell, hitting her head hard on the couch next to her. When she came around Jai was holding her hand, and Anil was holding a distraught Meera.

Nikki turned on her stomach on Meera's bed. *Oh my Meera, I miss your presence next to me. You knew when I had a headache coming on; you knew when I got cranky before my period. I miss your touch, your warmth, my child. I miss your hand holding mine when I am watching TV, I miss the kisses you would shower on me when you hugged me from the back. I failed you, I could not get more life for you, I could not give you mine. I would, you know, a hundred times over.*

In the initial days, Meera had the optimism of the young. At 16, you think you are immortal, because old age seems so far away. There is invincibility, a feeling that you are unique, you will not be impacted with what afflicts others. So you could try drugs because you are stronger than anyone and will not succumb to its pleasures. You can drive a bike at high speed and you won't meet with an accident because you are a dude. At that age, the possibilities of what you can do are endless, and there is no stopping you. Meera was confident that her young healthy body would not let her down. That it would fight back. That she would not die.

She pestered Nikki and Anil. 'Are you sure the doctor read my test reports? What if he is wrong? Shouldn't we see another doctor? How can this happen to me?'

The first two weeks after Meera's diagnosis were a haze. Those days are a blur in Nikki's mind now. All she remembers is endless conversations with numerous doctors, discussions with family members who were constantly there with them. Her brother Anand and his wife Piya went to all the doctors with them, while Piya's brother, KD, managed to get them early appointments because of his network in the industry. First opinion, second, third, and fourth opinions, innumerable appointments. They were always waiting at the doctor's chambers to meet someone. The verdict never changed. Meera was not going to live long.

Finally in despair one day, Jai spoke up. 'Can't you see Meera has little time with us? Shouldn't we all be together instead of spending time meeting doctors who tell us the same thing?'

That stopped the whole family in its tracks. It took a 13-year-old to make them face the truth—and to accept the inevitable.

That day, Nikki took Meera out for a coffee at the Coffee Day on Carter Road. It had been years since they had gone out for a coffee together, because now the teenage Meera went there with her friends to hang out instead.

They were lucky and got a table just by the sidewalk. It was a lovely November evening, and the weather was just perfect—no humidity, cool and breezy. Nikki ordered her cappuccino and Meera went with a peach iced tea. They both sat observing other people and then Nikki spoke to Meera.

'Have you considered how lucky you are Meera?'

Meera glared at Nikki with a shocked expression. 'Ya right Mom. I am super lucky. I have a malignant tumor and I am going to die soon. But I am very lucky.'

Bad choice of words. Nikki saw her agitation but remained calm. 'Look at the blessing Meera. You may have not had any time at all. People die all the time. Of accidents, of heart attacks that creep up on them suddenly, of diseases that are never diagnosed. I could die tomorrow in an accident and never be able to tell you I love you. I know it is terrible, but you have advance notice. You know you have little time left. So you need to live it to the fullest. Do everything you want to do, meet who you want to, tell people who bother you what you think of them, make up with people you love, and be happy.'

Meera looked at Nikki with tears in her eyes. In a small voice she said, 'I don't want to die Mom. I wanted to do so many things.'

Nikki's heart cried, but she knew she had to be strong. Meera would lean on her for strength and courage. *This time I cannot let my child down. I have to hold myself, hold her. Hold all of us together.* 'I know, my love. If there was anything I could do to keep you with me forever I would do it. I cannot even begin to fathom what I will do without you. But that is the reality we all are living with. So let's do what we can with it.'

Meera looked away towards the sea. She remained silent for the longest time, but Nikki did not want to disturb her train of thought. The sun had set already and the streetlights had come on. But there was no lull in the traffic or the people milling around. The breeze was even cooler now. After an eternity, Meera looked at her and smiled wanly, 'You are right Mom. We could make a list of things I want to do.'

That list, prepared on coffee-shop napkins was now framed, and Nikki put it up in Meera's room. In her darkest moments, she would look at the list and smile, then cry and remember. Somehow, for a short time, the list would dispel her despair.

Meera's to-do list

✓	go to see the Northern Lights in Norway
✓	See a play on Broadway or in London
✓	Eat loads of Chinese food from China Gate
	Have sleepovers with friends
✓	have a super 16th birthday party
✓	distribute my clothes among my friends
✓	leave my iPod for Jai
✓	Read all John Green books
✓	See all Karan Johar movies again
✓	Meet Ranbir Kapoor
✓	Drive a car at least once
✓	taste beer
✓	taste wine
✓	eat crabs at Mahesh lunch home
✓	sit in a limousine
	go for a Justin Bieber concert
✓	kiss Mom and Dad - a lot
✓	fight with Jai
✓	Bake a cake
✓	Learn a song on the guitar
	Get my first kiss
	Get a report card with all As and A+s
	Tell AJ I like him
	Tell Gitika I hate her because AJ likes her

All those with tick marks were the ones Meera managed to do.

Meera's last birthday. She was worried that she would feel sick but the day dawned perfectly for her, almost as if a power up there wanted her to enjoy the day to her fullest. As a concession to Jai, she 'allowed' him to get two more friends to her party.

How gorgeous my love looked that day! And how she glowed and beamed. Her entire class and all her friends had turned up for the party. And Meera danced and danced the whole night.

Mid-December, the family left for London. The dreary, gloomy London weather did not dampen their happiness. They watched *The Lion King* at the Lyceum Theatre and Nikki and Anil had tears in their eyes as they sang 'Circle of Life' together. Meera wanted to shop at London and Nikki did not have the heart to tell her that those things would be just memories in a few months. From London, they proceeded to Tromso in Norway and were lucky to see the Northern Lights. That night at Ersfjorden, as they saw the spectacular lights over the fjord and the surrounding hills, Nikki felt a peace descend on her. All bundled up in her clothes, Meera's face was shining, happy, and alive.

If our lives are a sum total of our experiences, then at least Meera has had a lucky one. In her brief life, she has lived it to the fullest. That is a blessing too.

After the Europe trip, Meera was in a lot of pain on most days, and the doctors put her on heavy doses of steroids to ease her pain. She wanted to rest a lot more too, and some days she would miss school. The school had been generous in accommodating Meera. She was allowed to come late and was also allowed to leave early if she was feeling sick. Nikki would cajole her to get out of bed and go to school. On days that Meera stayed back, Nikki would not go to office and would lie down next to her. They caught up on all the Karan Johar and Ranbir Kapoor movies. Meera wanted to listen to all her childhood stories over and over again and Nikki would narrate them on demand. Meera told Nikki things that she had not told her earlier. Like how she had crushed on a boy in school and he had not even paid her the slightest attention. How she thought she was unattractive because she was so tall. How she hated her boobs. How her first thought when she studied reproduction was 'Eeow!

That's what my parents did!? Disgusting.' How once she had taken money out of Nikki's purse to buy her flowers on her birthday. How she loved to trouble Jai and got his secrets from his friends.

In the evenings, the family would sit together and watch TV shows. In those months they caught up on *24, Grey's Anatomy, Friends,* and *How I Met Your Mother.* Anil gave Meera her first taste of beer and wine while Jai took her pictures. Her face had contorted into an unrecognizable mass and was beetroot red!

When Meera breathed her last, Piya took charge. Nikki remembered very little of those days. Her moment of extreme distress was when Meera was bathed and they made her wear a pretty pink *salwar kameez.* Meera looked so beautiful. Rested. All the pain was gone from her face. There was *kirtan* at home, but even the soothing *kirtans* and recitals from the Guru Granth Sahib did not penetrate the dark gloom in Nikki's heart. She felt like a part of her heart had been torn away from her, and there was an empty cavity in her heart that seemed to be filled with a dark, viscous grief that refused to flow out.

When the school called and asked Anil if they could have a memorial service for Meera, Nikki did not know what to expect.

Nikki felt her feet give way when they arrived at the school. She leaned on Anil and saw his ashen face. This was as difficult for him, yet he supported them both. At the school gate, Nikki pictured Meera standing there, all of four years old, on her first day of school. Ever since she had gone there for a teacher–student interaction six months prior to her acceptance at the school, Meera had wanted to go back there. She had refused to go to her pre-school because she liked the 'big' school more. On the first day of school, despite being the fussy eater that she was, Meera literally gulped down her food in her excitement. She looked angelic in her pigtails and the blue uniform. As they entered the school, Meera suddenly felt nervous and held on tightly to Nikki's hand. But when Ms. Benazir, the school supervisor, walked up to her and said, 'Let's go to our new class, Meera,' she immediately let go of Nikki's hand and caught Benazir's little finger.

'My baby didn't even look back. And I didn't even manage to kiss her in that moment,' Nikki told Anil, and he smiled and said, 'Wait and watch darling!'

Nikki barely registered the huge numbers of students who had turned up for the memorial service. Meera's best friends, Dev, Kajal and Sammy, came up to her. Nikki hugged them tight and even though she had promised herself to be dignified, tears rolled down her cheeks. These children had been with Meera every single evening since her diagnosis. One of them, or two, or all three, would come over after school and tell Meera all that had happened in school. That day, at the memorial service, they were as distraught as she was.

When we are young, we think we are invincible. And immortal. That death cannot touch us. And that we can conquer anything at all. But then, suddenly, when death comes visiting and takes one of your closest pals, it shatters you completely.

Most of the memorial was a haze for Nikki. She looked at the teachers and the students and tried to be gracious as they came up to her to offer their condolences.

These kids are smarter than me. I still don't know what to say to someone when a close one passes on. And there are times when I have not picked up the phone to commiserate with someone because I didn't know what to say.

The principal spoke. Her teachers spoke. Meera was a straight-A student and well liked by her teachers. She was a diligent student and always made sure her submissions were on time. She was on the school magazine's editorial team and the English teacher read out an unpublished poem Meera had written.

I have my memories, but so many of these people hold memories of Meera too. Today she is on their minds, but tomorrow, they will get busy and she won't be anymore. The teachers will have new favorites, the school magazine will have another contributor, and the children will grow up, make friends, and lead their lives. Meera will become a memory, one that surfaces once in a while. And then, suddenly, no one will remember her anymore because there will be no new memories to add. Will I forget my child too?

Nikki was bursting with pain. This was not a good idea. She did not want to be around those kids, in that school. It was too vivid a reminder of Meera. She should have felt grateful, instead, she was feeling resentful, angry, and extremely bitter. All this was a really bad joke. It would not do to show her ingratitude, so Nikki blanked out and thought of nothing. She focused on Meera's large portrait in the front—smiling that beautiful smile that could light up any room. So when she first heard Meera calling out to her, Nikki thought she was delusional. She was jolted out of her blankness and then heard Meera's voice again. Nikki's eyes went wild as they scanned the big hall for Meera.

And found her on the big screen. In a video shot by her friends. Meera was sitting on her bed. *So this is what they had been doing behind her closed bedroom door!* This must have been around three weeks before her death, because Meera's eyes were sunken low in her sallow face. She was wearing the Hermès scarf she had picked up on the London trip.

Nikki watched in shock as the recording unfolded. Meera and her friends had picked up pictures and video recordings of the family over the years to put together this farewell gift that Meera had left for them. Pictures of Meera's on the day she was born, Meera's first steps, Meera smearing Jai with chocolate cake, Meera singing 'Sound of Music' on the hills of Mussoorie, Meera in a cast with a broken foot, Meera with her friends, Meera eating *pani puri*, Meera modeling her new clothes. Meera lying in bed in her last days and filming the family and all her friends who came to visit her. Her meeting with Ranbir Kapoor that KD managed to swing for her.

And Nikki smiled, and cried, and smiled and cried.

A mother does not nourish her children. Her children nourish her. They feed her love, they feed her attention, warmth. They become the reason for her existence. The reason for her sleepless nights. The reason for her terror—terror that something will go wrong with them, that they will get lost, that someone will take advantage of them, that they will fall into bad company, that they will lose focus, that they will not grow into good human beings. They become the reason for her strength; they help her go through life. Help her get over failures. Help her fight and emerge stronger and surer of herself. They help her become a better person because she does not want to look small in their eyes.

Nikki had memorized all that Meera said in the video:

Mom and Dad. And my darling Jai. By the time you see this, I will be long gone. We—Dev, Sammy and Kajal—thought this up for you. I want you to know how much I love you. And how glad I am that I was born as your daughter. I love the warmth of your hugs, Mom, and the lovely way you smile when you have a secret up your sleeve. I used to love the days you were home and would be there to hug me when I got back from school. I love the Maggi you make. I loved the way you would suddenly lose energy and get tired. And I loved watching all the silly movies with you. And I know you would have been cool if I had gotten a boyfriend. I would like to have been a mom like you if I had grown up. And oh yes, I love the way you abuse when things don't go your way. And I always liked to snuggle into your bed and feel your warmth. Don't lose weight mom—you rock.

Dad. My sweetie cutie. You are such a softie. I know you wanted me to play football, but seriously, the ball never connected with my foot! I love the way you snore, and the way you would come in after a party to kiss me. I wanted to grow up and buy you a Mercedes. And I was going to be a smart MBA with a great salary and I would go to the US to work. And I would send business class tickets for Mom and you to come visit me. But now I can't. Take care of Mom, Dad, and go out on your romantic dinners. I love you.

Jai. I hate you. I hate the fact that you are such a cool dude and all my friends have a crush on you. I hate the way you make studies look so simple and do so well at sports too. The only time I barely liked you was when it was Rakhi and I would get a gift from you. I like that girl of yours though. I always wanted to be like you. Popular, smart—you are a great bro! And btw, you can find your iPod in the last drawer of my study table. And the band your girl gave you in my jewelry case. And yes, I know your passwords, but shan't say them here. Will miss you bro. Love you. Miss me, because I will miss you all too. And don't forget me!

Meera had left recordings for her best pals too, and Nikki hoped they would cherish those for a lifetime.

In her grief, Nikki registered Jai's attempts to reach out to her. He would come from school and sit with her on the bed and watch mindless TV with her. He would tell her of all the inane things he did at school. He declined sleepovers to his friends' houses because he did not want to leave Nikki alone. Through the gloom of her heart, Nikki recognized all this. She did not want him to do all that. She did not want him to stop living. She did not want him to think he was responsible for her happiness. She knew he hurt for Meera too. They fought like crazy but they crazily bonded too. Meera would look out for him and he was protective about her. Rakhi would be hollow for him this year, even though Piya's daughters would come over. She knew he would be sad that day. On Rakhi, Nikki would give them money and they all liked to go to the mall and buy candy for themselves and eat a meal together. Meera would always write a silly nonsensical poem on his birthday and Nikki thought that secretly, that was Jai's most cherished gift every year.

She was grateful for Jai coming into her bed in the morning and cuddling her. She was grateful for his voice that soothed her, though she did not register most of anything. She wanted his warmth—and wanted to hold on to it.

Nikki kissed Meera's pillow and got out of bed. She smoothed the sheet. It had been six months since Meera had left them, and the pain had not eased. But there was Jai and Anil. And her Meera, who lived in her every moment of every day.

Nikki smiled sadly. *They lie when they say time heals everything. It does not. We merely become better at handling the pain. It is about time I made Jai's favorite risotto. And went to fetch him from school. And took him for a movie. And listened to him. My Jai is still with me. I need to be his mom again.*

Veera

'Have you spoken to Namita? She has not taken my calls, or even Mana's. Where the hell is the woman? She should be here,' I hear KD say.

'I have been on email with her. She is at that Karjat shoot of hers, and will be back this weekend, hopefully,' Piya responds. She is sitting next to me. I can feel her filing my nails. I bet she is putting red nail paint on me. She knows I love it, and am sure she hopes I will appreciate it when I get up.

—She has pissed me off big time Piya. Not turning up when Mom is in the hospital. The girl has to know when to give up the fight.

—KD, let her be. You know they have had many issues. Namita has to resolve them.

—I don't understand how she can hold things against Mom. Yes, we all fight, but that does not mean we don't stand up for each other or stand with each other when there is a crisis. Sometimes you women just harbor so much anger.

Piya says nothing. I want to tell KD I understand my Namita. I know she will come. She is the gentlest of all my three kids. A sensitive child, and in my determination that she should not suffer like I have, I have been harsh with her. She in turn has done everything to anger me. Cutting that beautiful, long, curly hair. I used to love her hair. I would massage it with warm coconut oil every day. I used to buy the expensive Johnson's baby shampoo for her hair. It was difficult to comb it out, but we usually didn't do it. Her curls used to dry out and frame her face so beautifully. And then she went and chopped it all. Even boys have hair longer than hers. Her excuse—she did not want to fuss about her hair when she was out shooting.

And staying in the same apartment with that boy Atul? She did that deliberately, because she knew I would be furious. Which decent girl stays in a house with a boy who is not her husband? She says Atul is not her boyfriend either.

I don't understand these things. I try to learn and be modern, but I can't understand. These are the reasons she hasn't been able to find a good boy and get married. Which boy will want to marry a used product? She gets angry when I say this, but it is the truth.

When my children discuss today's generation, they always say things like, 'Mom, times have changed. Girls and boys go out together. They can be friends.' Or, 'Live-in relationships are common.' And Piya and KD justify Atul staying with Namita: 'Look at it this way. There is someone at home to take care of her. She is not alone in that big apartment.' They are convinced that Atul is not her boyfriend, or out to use her. They have been friends for a long time, and Atul has a girlfriend in Delhi.

I tell them people don't change. There have been changes in our society, but these are superficial. Deep down, we are still constricted by the chains that have bound us forever. Why should I talk of anyone else, when I am old-fashioned in many ways? I have led an independent life, but I would not have liked KD to marry a girl he chose himself. To bring me a girlfriend that he wanted to marry. It is important to get the right girl into your house. One who will fit in and take your value system as her own. In India, you marry the family, so it was important for me to find the ideal person for our family. No matter how liberal guys are, they still want to believe that their wives are virgins on their first night. The girls who boys like to date are not the ones they marry. Men can have affairs and pre-marital sex; women cannot.

They don't see it now, but when my grandchildren are older, I want to see how differently my own children will behave.

In life, the more things change, the more they remain the same.

In this sterile hospital room, I miss the sounds of my house. The early-morning alarm that wakes up Mana. Her calls to the maids to get up. The sound of her gentle love as she wakes up my grandchildren for school. Soon the quiet is shattered. The kids fight over the slightest thing, Mana scolds them for not eating, KD gets into an argument with Ranvir, Mana exhorts the maids to hurry with the tea, the tiffins. The doorbell rings incessantly as the car cleaner, the driver, the *dhobi*, the newspaper guy, and other sundry people begin their day. I get up and sit and cajole the kids to eat, chat with KD, and drink my tea. When the kids and KD leave, Mana and I get some time together. We sit together, drink our tea, and have our breakfast. We discuss the catering assignments for the day and before long, the madness of the day begins again.

I heard the doctors come into the room the other day. I don't understand medical terms too well, but from what I could understand, they think when I fell, my head hit the bathroom tiles in such a manner that I passed out immediately. There was internal bleeding. Aneurysm, I think is the word they used. KD worries. A ruptured aneurysm can cause death. He worries that I will not wake up from my coma. That I will die.

I want to tell KD, Death is His own master. Death comes when He wants to. And when He is ready for you, no matter what you do, He will take you. No amount of prayers will save you then. Death will come for me when it is time; else He would have taken me years ago, when as a young, married girl, I prayed for Him to come take me.

The unhappiness of those years was too much to bear for my tiny 13-year-old body. Married to a person who did not ever talk to me and who only wanted me in bed to satisfy his urges. Stuck in a house where I had no friends. No one I could talk to. No one who cared about me.

Do you know how it feels? To be unloved, unwanted, uncared for? When no one cares to ask you if you want a favorite dish cooked? When you eat the leftovers in the end? When you are not allowed to participate in any discussion? When you cannot offer an opinion? When you get your period and your stomach hurts, and you get a tight slap on your face because people think you are feigning illness to avoid work?

I was pampered in my mother's house. Even through all the pain of the Partition, I was loved. We lost Nimmi and *beyji* was haunted by guilt and remorse. But they loved me, and *bauji* still bought me candy or trinkets with the little money he had. On my wedding day, Veerji gave me a little radio. He knew how much I loved music.

I did not care about the gold trinkets that *maaji* took away from me and kept aside as dowry for her unmarried girls. I did not care when my sisters-in-law took the five beautiful saris my mother had lovingly collected for my wedding. They chose who would add what to her dowry. I did not even care when I was given three cotton suits that were my clothes for the year. But I cried noiselessly for days when *maaji* took away my radio. I loved it. It was mine. Veerji had given it to me. There was no one to listen to my weeping or to care about wiping my tears away. It is a lonely feeling, when you don't matter to anyone. That your tears and sorrow mean nothing to the people you live with. That the people who care about you are so far away.

Every year, for 14 years before I finally conceived KD, I prayed. I prayed for a boy. I prayed for a healthy boy. I prayed for a boy who would live.

My womb did not support me. It did not support the child in my womb. Every year, I would go through nine months and then excruciating labor—only to deliver a stillborn child, or a child who would die soon after. The cursed womb lay heavy on me. It created another wall between Gurujitji and me. *Baaji* used to say that after a woman delivered her baby, the womb would hurt, because it was seeking the baby it had nurtured for nine months. And when it seeks it hurts. My womb hurt me so much and cried in helpless frustration too. And I had nothing to hold on to.

Imagine being pregnant every year. And then delivering stillborns or children who would not survive. It eats you up, inside and outside. I used to feel like my innards were being scraped all the time. As if there were worms in my body eating me up, eating my babies.

It's unimaginable, the emotional trauma of losing the child you carry with so much expectation. Of the dreams you weave around them. Of the pain of seeing someone else with her little baby. Of a happy family cooing over an infant. Of the pitter-patter of little feet. And the words that were hurled at me—they have the power to shake me up even today. *Baanj, khasma nu khaani, marjaani, kalmuhi.* The furtive whispers in my family and the looks I got at social gatherings. People slithered away from me as if I was an untouchable, an ill omen. As if I would eat the infants born to other women. As if my shadow would curse a newlywed couple, who would not be able to conceive because of my evil eye. *Maaji* stopped taking me out with her. It was a relief to be away from those accusing eyes.

My failure clung to me like second skin. *Maaji's* agitation with me knew no bounds. She wanted Gurujitji to send me back home. Wanted him to marry again. I did not see the mirror for many days, because I only saw a failed woman. One who was not loved by her husband and one who could not satisfy him. Like she had failed to deliver the promised dowry, she had also failed in her duty to bear him a child.

Gurujitji, however, declined to get married again and was adamant about it. He was honor-bound to be committed to me. I know he never loved me, and I did not love him either, but this act of kindness bound me to him and my respect for him was immense. That kindness helped me tide over the torture and mental abuse *maaji* doled out.

I never told my children what *maaji* did to me. After every delivery, she would throw out the part-time help. I would sweep, mop, clean, iron, wash...my days were an endless haze. She would not let me eat with the rest of the family. And Gurujitji, the obedient son, never even noticed. He had been brought up in an environment where the women ate after the men of the family had finished their meal. I wonder if he ever knew I was given only two *rotis* and *dal* and *sabzi*. Never a dessert. Never sugar in my tea. And I never got to eat any fruit, even the ones that Veerji brought for me. Veerji always brought me mangoes when they were in season. He knew I loved them so.

In Rawalpindi we had so much fun with mangoes. When the trees bore fruit, we would wait impatiently for the *kairi*—raw mango—that *beyji* would cut into thin slices and season with salt and red chillies. I remember the long, seemingly endless afternoons of sitting with my cousins and licking, sucking and eating *kairi*. My teeth always felt tender and sour after eating so much *kairi*, but it was such a pleasure. When mango season was in full bloom, there were so many varieties of mangoes to choose from. *Totapuri, langda, safeda, dussheri, sindoori,* and *malda*. All the mangoes were put in a big steel tub full of water and left to cool in a shady corner of the courtyard. After every meal, we would eat mangoes. I used to eat them with my bare hands, biting off the top with a long breath and then sucking the mango dry. Later, after I had literally eaten the skin thin, I would suck and suck at the seed till it was devoid of any flesh or flavor. The adults would make fun of me because my seed would be white, with not a speck of the mango flesh anywhere.

Then there was always *aam panna* at home in the hot summer days. The green raw mangoes would be boiled, mashed, and mixed with sugar, rock salt, and cumin. Add one part of this to four parts of water, and you had a refreshing, cooling drink ready. Along with *nimbu pani*, this was a staple drink in our Rawalpindi home in the summers.

I loved mango pickle too. In those summer months, making the mango pickle was an elaborate process, and one that everyone in the house enjoyed. Every year, small farmers from around Rawalpindi would come town and go door-to-door with their harvest of raw mangoes. *Baaji* had a good eye for the best mangoes for pickles. She would sit on a chair in the courtyard, while the vendor laid out his mangoes. She would touch and feel each mango before setting it aside. Then, as the vendor sat drinking the tea or *lassi* that was offered to him, the servants would wash each mango with care and dry it with a clean cloth. The vendor would then take out his sharp blade and cut each mango into pieces—*baaji* dictated the size of each piece. She usually liked them to be about a square inch. Soon, there would be a little mound of cut mango pieces, which would be a sign for us kids to begin our game. We would sneak pieces of the mangoes and run away with them. God forbid if *baaji* caught us though—we would then be subjected to some painful ear pulling.

That day, the mangoes were left in the big flat pans to dry. The next morning, the air would be redolent with the smells of the spices that went into making the pickle. The process of making a mango pickle even today transports me back to those idyllic times. The heady aroma of mustard oil, fenugreek seeds, and fennel seeds. When the mixing was done, *baaji* would supervise the filling of the stone *martabans* with the pickle. I never quite understood why women who were menstruating were not allowed to touch pickle—at any stage of its life. When I asked *beyji*, she told me that women had a special secretion at that time that spoiled the pickle. I don't know if that is true or not, but I still believe it!

Once, when Veerji came visiting with *dussheri* mangoes, he asked me to eat a mango with him. I hesitated because I could feel *maaji's* seething disapproval. But Gurujitji was at home that day and he told me to eat one with them. I can't tell you the excitement I felt. I almost quivered with pleasure and imagined how the mango would feel on my tongue. And it felt as good as I had imagined it to be. Oh how I had missed the sweet, juicy, yellow flesh. We laughed—Veerji, Gurujitji and I—when I gobbled up the mango greedily.

I paid for it the next day. *Maaji* thrashed me for eating the mango with such relish. '*Kalmuhi*, have you no shame? Eating like a hungry dog? As if we starve you!' But thereafter, every single year when Veerji came with the mangoes, I would eat one. I figured it was alright to be beaten afterwards for that mango—the one thing that gave me pleasure.

After the third time I failed to deliver a healthy baby, when Veerji came home, he asked *maaji* if he could take me to Delhi and get me checked by a doctor. She glared at him as if he had blamed her for my health. She was curt and said, 'Jarnail Singhji. Are you suggesting that we don't take good care of your sister?'

'No *ji*, that was not what I meant. This would also be an opportunity for Veera to meet our mother. It has been three years since she came home.'

Maaji's eyes went cold as she politely said, 'Okay, you can take her. And bring her back when she is well again.'

My heart froze. *Maaji* wanted me out of Gurujitji's life. She would never let me come back to this house again. She would get him married. I could not leave.

I told Veerji, 'Veerji, I am doing well. *Maaji* takes good care of me. Tell *beyji* I will come home next year.'

Veerji's eyes were hurt and furious. How could I tell him what the problem was? It was not as though he could do anything about it. These days when young people want a divorce because they can't live together, I only shake my head helplessly. What do they know of incompatibility? Of living with people who dislike you and who won't let you meet your parents? Who treat you so badly that you lose all your self-respect. In our days, we didn't even think of these things. I could not bring shame upon my parents. When they married me to Gurujitji, they waived all their rights over me. My in-laws could choose to do what they wanted with me. Educate me, make me work outside, or keep me locked up behind closed doors and never let me see my parents again. If I had gone back with Veerji that day, the doors to Gurujitji's house would have been closed to me forever. And I would have had nowhere to go. No one would have married me—a used woman with a barren womb.

I am sure my family knew of the ill-treatment that was being meted out to me, and they must have felt remorse. To have lost Nimmi to the riots in Rawalpindi because her in-laws and husband refused to move to India, and then to lose the second daughter to a bad marriage.

But our times were such that there was nothing they could do. Today, young girls have it so much better. Look at Piya and Mana. They are equal to their husbands, they have the freedom to have careers and make friends. When we sit at the dining table, they get into arguments with their husbands. We were not allowed so much freedom. Of course, no one compares to Namita—married to her job and many boyfriends!

My parents never came to meet me. Perhaps they felt shame. Or maybe Mumbai was too far away. Veerji came every year. He would get pictures for me to see. Sepia-toned pictures of my parents, of Veerji's family, and my nieces and nephews. He would press money in my hands and whisper that it was for me alone. And he would tell me of the piece of jewelry *beyji* bought for me, and would give me when I went to meet them in Delhi.

Veerji's visits always cheered me up, and then left me depressed for days on end. I longed to go home. Longed to be with my own people. Longed for a friendly hug, a kind smile, a meal that someone cooked for me with love. It was years before I saw my parents again.

KD's daughter, Rishika loves to feel my face. With her tiny fingers, she outlines each wrinkle on it. Once, she wanted to know how I had got these lines on my face.

I told her that each wrinkle of mine has a story to tell. The deep one on my forehead was when KD was 10. He fell down while playing cricket, and broke open his skull. We rushed him to Holy Family Hospital. I remember those horrible days. He was so small, with tubes running through his frail body—IV lines for food, for medicines. I sat next to my son all day and night, for weeks. I had not done *path* since I had come to Mumbai. Miraculously, after 20 years or more, I still remembered it. I recited *Japji Sahib, Rehras,* and *Anand Sahib* from memory. I would go to the Dhan Potohar

Gurudwara and pray in front of the Guru Granth Sahib. I promised Babaji everything—I would not eat meat, I would not wear new clothes for a year, and I would give up pink which was my favorite color. I would not eat ice cream again because KD loved it. I would not watch any movies. I would never think bad thoughts about *maaji*. I prayed to Babaji to let KD live. He was my happiness, my deliverance from sorrow—a long spate of sorrows—a bad marriage, stillborn babies, a life shorn of happiness.

Of course I did not tell Rishika all these things. May her destiny be better. The smart girl asked me why I still eat chicken and ice cream when I had sworn to not do so. I told her that those promises were only for a year. When she grows up she will know that the promises that are broken are the sweetest.

And this other wrinkle. When Namita got pregnant and Kal refused to marry her. How much had I told her he was one sleazy fellow. It was obvious to me from the beginning that he was charmed by her nature, by what he thought was a 'fast' girl. He wanted to curry favor with KD. I never liked him. He would have a drink when he came over to our house, but he would not drink in front of his father. Kal's brother would not drink in front of him. This hypocrisy always bothered me. A man who does not have the courage to follow his heart—that fool was not meant for my daughter. She deserved much better. Namita cried and cried. I hurt so much for her, but I wasn't able to tell her that. I was very harsh with her. I don't think she has forgiven me for that. If I could rewind back to that time, I would behave better. I would still pick up the phone and blast that *haraami* fellow. But I would hold Namita and kiss her. I would not let her go to the doctor all by herself for that abortion.

When lines started appearing on my face, I felt very depressed. I had only just begun to live my life and the mirror told me I was an old woman already. When I was young and pretty (so they tell me), I had never looked at myself in the mirror with pleasure. Now the mirror mocked me.

Then, some years ago, Piya had come visiting and was lying down on my bed as I got ready for dinner. She watched me, as she had as a young girl too. She saw me tie my hair up in a bun, wear my *kajal*, and lipstick, and she commented, 'Mom, you have grown into a very elegant woman. You look so charming and gracious.' She came and hugged me from behind. In the mirror, I saw two faces. Of my beautiful young daughter in the prime of her youth, and mine, with its lines and thinning hair. And eyes that had seen a lifetime.

That day, a cloud lifted from my heart. I looked at myself in the mirror again, and saw myself through Piya's eyes. And I did look beautiful. My face looked like the face of a woman who has seen the world—its beauty and cruelty—and emerged a winner. I fell in love with myself again.

Namita

To: namitak@gmail.com
From: Piyar@gmail.com
Jun 26, 2013
1 p.m.

My college professor once asked our class if parents brought up each child in the family in the same manner, or if they brought them up differently. I argued that each child was brought up in the same manner. After all, parents love each child and the assets are there to be shared by everyone. You will feed the children the same food, give them the same education, and have the same expectations from each.

Now that I am a parent, I realize the foolishness, or shall we say, immaturity of my reaction. I can see Mom loved us all, but had different expectations from each of us. KD is the son of the family, and he was expected to take on the mantel of being the man of the house. So when KD established himself at work, he first bought the Samshiba apartment for Mom and Mana on Pali Hill. Then he got me married, and as a gift I was given the Apsara apartment. The very same year, he gifted you the apartment in Nibbana. Did he have a choice, you think? Thankfully he has done so well, but imagine the pressure on *bhai*.

I think Mom leaned on you emotionally, as her older daughter. She always wanted you to be impeccable—in your dressing, in the way you spoke, and in the way you conducted yourself. I can imagine the burden of her constant criticism. I do the same with Garima. I try to pull back, but I want her to be the best, Namita. I get angry with her if I see her watching TV or chatting with her friends. Left to me, that poor child would be studying all the time. I don't give her any leeway when she is rude or gets grades less than an A, and I punish her with long silences.

Contrast that with the way I am with Aditi. Nothing she does agitates me. When she is rude or throws a tantrum I feel like hugging and kissing her. She is my toy. Truthfully, I don't pay any attention to her achievements, so I am constantly surprised when she does well—in academics or sports.

I think that is the way Mom was with me. And that's why I view her differently. But this I can tell you Namita, what she did for you, she would not do for me or even KD.

I have a very vivid memory of her making *gulab jamuns*. You were in college, and KD was whiling away time; he was to leave for his MBA in two weeks. She used to love to make them from scratch. In the afternoon, when she was done with her work, she got together the ingredients to make them. KD and I were hovering in the kitchen because we both wanted milk powder. Remember how we used to take spoonfuls of Lactogen in our mouths? It would get stuck to the palate of our mouth, and then we would remove little bits of it with our tongue and enjoy the sickly sweet milk. (I used to do that when I got Lactogen for my girls too!)

Mom was just about done with deep frying those spongy milky balls and was dunking them into the sugary syrup. KD came up behind her and hugged her, and said, 'Give me the first one my sweet sweet Mom.' She smiled and said, 'Go away KD. Today Namita gets the first one. She loves these *gulab jamuns* and I have made them especially for her.' '*Accha*, so you will deny your only son? The heir to your family name?' joked KD. And she whacked his hand away and said, 'Yes my *jaan*. These are for my *dil ki dhadkan*.' I asked her what I was, if you were the *dil ki dhadkan* and KD was the *jaan*? She hugged me and said I was her *mishri*, the sweetness in her life.

KD and I teased her mercilessly. We told her she had it all wrong. You were the bitter *neem* in her life, and KD said he was the leech, because he was sucking all the money from her for his Harvard stay. She retorted that your bitterness was good for her health, else so much sweetness would give her diabetes. And waved the ladle at KD and joked, 'I expect my money back with a 1000 percent interest'. I wish you had been there to see her—she was seriously funny.

That evening, she was so excited because she wanted to see the delight on your face. And after dinner, when she took out the *gulab jamuns* and served you two in a bowl, you pushed the bowl away and remarked, 'I don't like them.'

I hated you then, Namita. Her face just collapsed like a deflated balloon and she silently gave the bowl to KD. She was quiet the whole evening after that. I don't know if you realized that she never made *gulab jamuns* at home again.

In those years, I thought Mom was very harried. She had the three of us in that already crowded little house, and so much work. She never gave any one of us breakfast. By the time we would get up, Mom would be ready. Remember she used to walk with us and then take the bus to the *mandi* with that Aarti *bai*? Mom used to keep bread, butter and jam on the table for us. On days that she was not very busy, she would also boil some eggs. And there was milk on the table that we could drink too. She was easy in the evening and we always got goodies to eat then. Remember? We would always ask her what she was cooking that day. That way we knew what was coming our way for dinner!

In her way, she wanted to make you happy. Maybe she did not have that much emotional bandwidth, but she tried to express it in the way she understood best.

To: Piyar@gmail.com
From: namitak@gmail.com
Jun 26, 2013
10 p.m.

How is Mom doing now? I dreamt of her last night. She was on her favorite sofa at home, sitting and sipping tea and saying something in English. I loved her story of how she learnt to speak in English. Do you remember it? That she knew only Punjabi and Hindi when she got married to Dad. She would try and make meaning of the words in the English newspaper that used to come home every day. When KD was born, she would take him for a walk in the evening, and would listen to people around her conversing in English. And one day, she mustered enough courage to speak to another lady with a baby. And according to Mom, she rehearsed her lines many times at home, in front of the mirror, before she told the lady in English, 'Your baby is beautiful. He looks just like you. What is his name?'

Today, can anyone tell Mom did not know how to speak in English till she was in her late 20s? For a woman of that era, she was really smart. I admire that about her. Perhaps that's the reason why I can't figure out why she would not let me do the things I wanted to do....

The shoot has been maddening. The rains have made the Western Ghats slippery and muddy. Sometimes we have to look for alternate routes because the torrential rains wipe out the route we had taken one way. I get really nervous about my camera being carted by this young village boy named Ram. He is like a mountain goat—sure-footed and fast. He has not slipped even once. And I keep falling all the time, making it down the mountain on my butt most of the time. By the time I get back to Karjat I look like a mess. Muddy and sometimes bloody too. So unladylike, as Mom would complain.

We must come to this farmhouse over a long weekend Piya. It is cozy and beautifully maintained. The landscaping is brilliant and the cook here is absolutely fabulous. Each evening, after we all take a bath, we meet in the living room. The room is lined with books. On one side it has a great bar and a big-screen TV on the other. We sit here till late night, looking at our work, planning the next day, and generally relaxing. It is so peaceful.

The trekking trails are magnificent—you will see them when they come in the magazine next month.

Strange! I have no memory of those *gulab jamuns*. And that's really upsetting me. Did I choose to remember only the bad things? I never thought I was the kind of person who saw the negative in people. I always take things in my stride. I am impatient, yes. Short-tempered, yes. But negative? I don't think so.

You know I tried to please Mom. Live up to her expectations. But I can't help the way I am, Piya. Even as kids, I could never sit still. I was always on the move. Do you remember? When my friends would dress up for parties and wear high heels, I was always in sneakers and they would make fun of me. It was difficult for me to explain to them that heels cramped my style. That I like walking fast. Mom wanted me to dress up in girlie clothes, but I was most comfortable in jeans and a t-shirt. In skirts, I would have to mind the way I sat. In jeans, I was myself and could sit anywhere, in any manner I wanted to. I couldn't cook to save my life. Remember how you threw away the eggs I once made? I was, and am, a disaster in the kitchen.

I studied hard, but I did not want to be a doctor or an engineer. I wanted to be a photographer. Of course I did not realize it then, that the temperament required for this career is so far removed from mine. Even after so many years. I cannot believe that this is the same me who can patiently wait till the tiger decides to make an appearance, or go without speaking for hours.

Piya

Three hundred more steps to take. Left. Right. Left. Right. That pain in the calves can wait. Left. Right. I need a sip of water. Not a good enough excuse to stop running. Left. Right. Come on Piya. Another two hundred to go. You can. If you can live without Him you can do anything. Left. Right. Another hundred to go. Breathe Piya. You are going on without Him. Waking up every morning with Him no longer there. Another fifty to go. Don't give up. Don't give up. There!

Piya stopped running as she approached the Taj Lands End at the very end of Bandstand. She was hot and sweaty and thirsty. And delighted. Today, she had managed to clock an hour of running without any break. A milestone achieved.

Running was her new passion. While running, she felt she had entered a meditative state. Ten minutes into running her mind blanked out all other thoughts. The only concerns were to put one foot in front of another, one step at a time, and to watch her breathing. She did not notice other people on the road, did not care if they noticed her.

Running eased the pain in her heart. Made her forget Him for a while. However brief, it was a welcome break...to not think of Him. Piya hunted out an empty bench and sat down on it.

You stay in a place like Mumbai and the avenues open for exercise and fitness are fairly limited. You could join the gym and pound the treadmill or the elliptical trainer every single day. Join Bollywood dance classes and move at impossible speeds to raunchy Bollywood songs. You can also contort your body at a yoga session—hot yoga, artistic yoga, Hatha yoga, there are many to choose from. Or Pilates, Krav Maga and Mallakhamb. Or anything that catches the fancy of Mumbai's elite.

After an intense day at work, the last thing Piya wanted to do was to get into a room with people she would be obliged to smile at or have a conversation with. The sweat-charged environment of those places usually made her gag. She did not want to go to any of them and make it a social outing. Besides, she loved the outdoors. Sure Mumbai does not have much of an outdoor to boast of, but Bandra is still a lovely place to walk. There are quiet lanes with sprawling bungalows, promenades like Bandstand and Carter Road, and parks with walking tracks—Joggers, Patwardhan, Rajesh Khanna, and Almeida. There are the hilly Mount Mary and Pali Hill that give the legs a wonderful workout. And of course the other busy Bandra roads where life is constantly on the move, and there is much to observe. Piya liked to see people on the roads, running errands, walking, de-stressing. She never walked with anyone. That was her time with herself.

Anand would tease her. Her walks did not reduce her carbon footprint. The driver would follow 'madam' when she went on her errands. There was no way she was going to carry loads of plastic bags from all that shopping she did while walking....

Who would have known that a friend request on FB would be the start of the most intense relationship of her life? When He sent her a friend request, it took her a minute to figure out who it was. The boy she remembered as her neighbor looked all grown up and different on FB. But when she figured who it was, it was an 'Aha' moment.

She was delighted. He was part of her gang on Chimbai Lane and they would all hang out together in the evenings. Three decades ago, there was not so much traffic in Bandra, and Mom did not mind her stepping out to spend time with her friends. A bunch of girls and guys would cycle together, walk on Bandstand or Carter Road and fight over *pani puri* and *bhel puri* at Hill Road. He would never talk to her directly, but only look at her with a smile on His face all the time. She had a crush on Him, but they both never got around to telling each other about it, even though the gang teased them both. Then, one day, He told her He liked her and wanted to date her. Deeply offended, she walked off in a huff and did not go out with the gang for a few weeks. She heard that His father was getting transferred to Delhi and she never saw Him or heard from Him again. She forgot Him, completely. Until now.

And He stayed right here, in Bandra, on Pali Hill. A few buildings away from her.

Funny that I never bumped into Him. Considering how small Pali Hill is, and the fact that we have a common circle of friends. And no one even thought of mentioning Him to me.

Thus started their conversation. It moved from FB, to emails, and then frequent calls. He told her things they had done. She didn't remember most of them, but little by little, bits and pieces of their lives together came back to her. Like Him waiting outside her tuition class so He could walk back home with her. Her calling Him home on the silliest of pretexts. Him gifting her cards that she promptly returned to Him. Her baking a cake on His birthday.

When Piya met Him for the first time at the Theobroma under her office, she was delighted. They chatted endlessly, about this, that, and the other. There was so much to talk about. Three decades to tell each other about, to fill in the gaps. He had branched out into software and now ran a company that was considered one of the best boutique firms in specialized software for healthcare insurance companies. He traveled a lot. His wife was an HR manager with a pharmaceutical company and they had two boys. He had moved back to Mumbai only a year ago from the US, and hadn't yet had the time to re-connect with old friends.

Life can be so funny. You forget people and then suddenly, memories come flooding back again. And you remember things with crystal clarity. Do I remember the events as they happened? Or do I choose to remember them as I wanted to retain them in my memory? There is no way to know if my memories are doctored—or mutated. If His version is the right one, or if mine is the one closer to truth. Or maybe it lies somewhere between the two.

He decided to join her for her walks whenever He could. They were connected the whole day through emails, SMSes, or calls, but Piya looked forward to those evenings when He was in Mumbai and could walk with her.

He drew her out of her naturally shy, reserved self. Piya found herself telling Him everything about herself. He seemed to get her, to understand what she felt, what she thought. He understood her journey and her choices. And he was non-judgmental about her. He was like Ayesha for Piya, and she felt herself incredibly drawn in, feeling intense closeness and attachment. And He told her everything. What He had done those past years, where He had gone, how He had met his wife, His business, His friends, His family, His likes, His dislikes...soon there was nothing she did not know about Him.

And slowly, steadily, Piya found herself falling in love with Him. He overwhelmed her with His attention and His desire for her. She wanted that touch from Him when they would be walking and accidentally bump into each other because of other people. Or when He would hold her lightly at the elbow when they had to cross the road.

One evening, walking together, they saw a little lane just before Nargis Dutt Road. It was barely visible, covered thick with vegetation. When they walked through it, it was as if they had entered another world altogether. The lane had no outlet; at its other end, the land suddenly ended and there was a stunning view of the Arabian Sea. Piya was awed. She had lived in the area all her life and never seen it. How had it remained hidden from the

Mumbai land sharks? They both stood at the very edge and watched the sun set. It was surreal, and when He turned to kiss her, it felt like the most natural thing in the world. His tongue felt unfamiliar in her mouth, but the hands that held and caressed her didn't feel strange at all.

And then He went on a long business trip to the US and was away for nearly two months. He was incorrigible. He wanted to talk to her at random hours. To escape Anand's attention, she would walk out of the house on flimsy pretexts. Sometimes it was to pick up veggies or some cheese or late at night, it would be to pick up meds for an imaginary ailment. If it was a dinner that they were catering for, Piya would pretend there was something that required her attention on location and escape.

How could a voice do it to me? His voice makes love to me—that slight American accent, the deep throaty laughter, the way He takes my name. 'Piya' never sounded more precious or beautiful. And I have not felt so loved, desired, wanted.

Piya had no clue when the relationship took a turn from a simple friendship to something deeper. Crazy it was. For three decades she had forgotten His existence, and now, He had entered her thoughts, had wormed his way into her blood, and had taken over her mind, her heart.

Then, one day He told her that He missed her terribly. That she was all He thought of. When He was in meetings, at official dinners, her face always sprung up in front of Him. He told her He wanted to travel with her, and see the world with her. He told her He loved her. That He had never stopped loving her.

He told her He was going to hug her tight and breathe her in deep, so He would always remember how she smelled. He told her He did not want her to wear perfume when she met Him next time.

And Piya dreamt of how He would hug her. And how she might fit in Him.

He told her He wanted to kiss her again. That He had wanted to kiss her every time they had met. He loved her smile and wanted to feel it under his own lips. He wanted to feel the softness of her lips and capture her smile.

And Piya dreamt of how He would kiss her. And of the pillowy sweetness of his full lips. Of the tongue that would be familiar now. He told her He wanted to touch her. Feel her body. Feel her warmth. He loved the way sweat clung to her face and body when they walked together and how He had resisted touching her, tasting her.

And Piya dreamt of how He would touch her, taste her. Piya felt herself go wet. Wet, as she had not been, in many years. She had forgotten that passion, that feeling, because frankly, how long could you lust after someone whose body was always available to you? She knew Anand and his moves down pat. She derived pleasure from the way Anand reached out for her and made her come—knowing when to touch, how to touch, and how long to touch.

But now, Piya ached. She felt wet and she ached...and ached for Him to relieve her.

Piya waited for Him to come back to Mumbai. For them to meet again. For Him to touch her. For her to touch Him and feel His body. He decided to return to the city a day before schedule. So He did not have to give His wife an explanation and Piya and He could be together. She told Anand that she had a girls' night out; Anand was used to her girlie nights. Ayesha and a bunch of other friends would meet at a bar and drink and make merry. Later, depending on how drunk they were, they would either go back to their respective homes, or move to someone's apartment and gossip and drink tea. Ayesha was in on her secret. She had known everything from day one. She would cover up for Piya if required.

Piya would remember the night at the Taj for the rest of her life.

Now, when Piya ran, she constantly agonized. *Did I have desperate written all over me? Did I come across as easily available in my happiness in connecting with him? In the way I spoke? In the way I expressed myself? Did I look like a slut? Easy to take to bed?*

Bandra felt claustrophobic to Piya now. The very same roads that brought her peace choked her. They were full of memories of her chats with him. Here, near Fabindia—she had asked Him how He spent time when He was at home, and He told her how He played with His boys, watched TV with them, chatted with His parents. Then suddenly He told her, 'Let's leave them all Piya, let's be together. You are the one I love.' And her heart had filled up with pure love for Him as she had laughed and said, 'You are crazy!'

Out running, Piya had once suddenly stopped in front of Rajesh Khanna Park. She had broken into a cold sweat. And remembered. This was where He had sent His first nasty SMS to her.

She had been out, expecting Him to call at his usual time. But He kept delaying it. And she kept following up with Him. Until He told her harshly that it was better that they stop talking all together. He could not take her pressure anymore. Piya's heart constricted as she remembered the shock. *She* was pressurizing *Him*? He, who called when He wanted to, at whatever time He wanted to? And did He not understand what trouble she went through?

Near PJ Club—where He had told her, 'It's been days since you told me you think of me or miss me. Don't you love me anymore?' Piya had smiled and said, 'Not really. It is my habit to talk to guys I don't love all the time.' He had retorted, 'Wait till I get my hands on you. This time, I won't let you breathe.' She had felt hot and wanted him right away.

Near the *bhel puri* guy on Pali Hill—when He had told her how His secretary would view Him with suspicion because He was on the phone so often and smiling and laughing into it. She was used to seeing Him stern. That ever since He had met Piya, His work was suffering. All He wanted was her.

At the grocery store near Zig Zag Road—when He had told her that she dominated His thoughts. That whether they spoke or not, she was always on His mind. Of how He looked forward to talking to her every day. He loved to listen to her voice, and loved listening to what she was thinking, what she was doing.

At Neelam Foodland—where He had told her He wanted her. Wanted to take a holiday to spend all alone with her. He could not get her off His mind. And even when He was working, He saw her—on His computer screen, in conversations with other people, and felt her presence next to Him all the time.

At Carter Road—when He had told her that she was being a fool. He had never promised her anything. Did she think He would leave his family because he had slept with her? That she was chasing Him and making Him hate her. He did not want to talk to her anymore.

At the gym—that she was a sick human being and was trying to blackmail Him. That He regretted ever meeting her. She was a nightmare.

A married man is a dangerous thing, Piya would think as she watched Anand. *They have learnt to handle a woman. Learnt what spots to touch to make a woman emotional. Learnt what to say to make her feel special. A married man can strum a woman like a guitar and tune her the way he wants to.*

That night at the Taj, he had already checked in and she went directly to His room. He opened the door, and smiled at her. Piya felt a certain nervousness and smiled hesitantly. She walked over to the windows to see the wonderful view of the sea from there.

He came up behind her and gathered her up in His arms. He kissed her. Slow and easy. She felt herself unwinding and relaxing into the warmth, the wetness, the love.

There was no room for conversation here. Or for foreplay. She sensed the hunger in Him and was as hungry for Him. They made love and as he moved above her, she looked at Him. She wanted to memorize His face. Her fingers traced the contours of His face. His smooth brow. His chiseled cheeks. His lips. The way His lips parted to reveal His teeth. And she wanted those lips all over her.

This is what heaven must feel like. And this is as close to divinity as I will ever come. He completes me, in ways that Anand or my kids don't. I don't think I could love anyone more, or be myself with anyone in the manner that I am with Him.

It was a night to remember. They made crazy love, showered together, and ate together. Laughed. Joked. Talked about their kids. Gossiped about close friends. Piya watched the way He ate, the careful way in which He cut the chicken and bit into it. The way He licked his lips after every few bites. And all of that made her wet, made her want Him more.

She snuggled into His arms, into the shoulder she loved and breathed in deep. *I never ever want to forget the way he smells.* She was finicky about smells and had a tough time adjusting to them. It took her forever to get accustomed to the way Anand smelled, but *this smell, I could get used to.* Piya ran her fingers over His body, wanting to commit every part of it to her memory so when He was not with her, she could draw it out in her mind and feel Him next to her. He looked at her and told her that she was all He had ever wanted. The kind of woman He wanted to marry. He pulled her into His arms and buried His face in her hair and said, 'I wish this was forever and I never had to leave you. You came back in my life three decades too late.'

Piya kissed Him and got out of bed. She looked out of the window, out to the sea front in front of the Taj. Lights glittered on it—from the ships docked out and boats that had party-goers in it. She loved parties on boats, except if she was with people that she did not like! Mumbai never sleeps and the front of the Taj looked like a *mela*. Late-night revelers hung around at the Gateway, getting pictures clicked. The balloon-sellers, *bhel puri* and *chai* vendors went from group to group peddling wares. She had heard that pimps and prostitutes also did brisk business here, but did not recognize the kind.

Piya turned to see Him on the bed. He was watching her. She said, 'You know the only thing I don't like? The fact that we will never hold hands in public. That we can't show affection in public. That the world will never know how much we love each other.'

He got out of bed. He looked gorgeous in His nakedness. He gathered Piya in His arms and kissed her. 'Why are you getting maudlin? We are together. That is all that matters.'

She snuggled into His arms and said, 'Your face, the one I love the most in this world, is not the one I wake up to every single morning. Your hand is not the one I will hold when I am distressed.'

He hugged her tight. And whispered in her ears, the heat of His breath filling her senses.

'Sweetheart, I know. I feel the same way. Yet, the way I look at it, I have found you again. And will not let you go. It may not be ideal, but it works for me. To know that you are in my life. And by the way, you belong to me. Totally. I am only loaning you out to Anand for this lifetime.'

Piya looked at Him. 'Does it bother you to know that Anand touches me? Does it make you jealous?'

He looked away. 'I don't think about it. I don't want to think about it because there is no point. I can't act on what I feel.'

Piya slept in His arms. Safe in the knowledge that she had her true love. A love that was hers alone. It was precious for her and had nothing to do with her being a mother, wife, daughter, sister, or any other role she played. There was no one she trusted more, and no one, apart from her kids, that she loved more. *Blessed is what I am.*

Piya smelled the smoke first. As she slowly came to consciousness, she saw Him sleeping next to her. She smiled at Him, immensely content to feel His warmth next to her, and kissed His lips. She made to get out of bed, and He reached out to her and kissed her. She felt Him grow hard against her, but distracted by the smell, she asked Him, 'Can you smell smoke?' He straightened up and said, 'Shit, is there a problem? I don't hear any alarms.'

Piya got out of bed and He warned her to not switch on the light. A spark could be dangerous. She opened the curtains a tad and saw fire engines outside. She quickly moved to call the hotel and picked up the phone. But it was dead.

Piya then saw her phone and the red notification light blinking. She had put it on silent, and now she saw loads of missed calls from Ayesha. And tons of messages.

In horror she began to understand what was happening.

'There are terrorists in the building! And they are killing people,' she told Him. He was stunned. 'Are you serious?!' She nodded her head dumbly and showed him the messages. 'Apparently they are covering this live on TV.'

She SMSed Ayesha asking her if she had told Anand. Ayesha replied in the affirmative.

What followed was a nightmare. Of trying to get out alive from that wretched place. Of thinking of her children and Anand. How was she going to face Anand? What would he say? What was she going to do?

In those harrowing hours Piya felt no fear. There was the business of surviving, of getting out alive. Of getting home to her kids. She held His hand and told Him, 'We will get out of this alive.' He nodded distractedly. 'What am I going to tell my wife, Piya? She will know I was with you. She has been suspecting for some time that I am involved with you.'

Piya hugged him, 'You have to say nothing to anyone. We will get out alive and no one need know we were together—ever.'

Piya opened the door, and a black cloud of smoke greeted her. She shut the door quickly. The corridor outside was like a gas chamber. There was no way they could use that route to escape. She panicked, wondering how in the world they were going to get out of the hotel. He came up with the idea of using wet towels on their heads to walk out. 'But what if we encounter a terrorist on our way out? We won't even know if they are there.' He said, 'Well, we have to risk it! Or we'll choke here anyway. Chances are that the terrorists have left the smoke-filled places.' He read the exit chart on the door as she got the towels wet and ready. Before they left, He held her close and kissed her. She asked him, 'You love me?' He smiled and said, 'To infinity.'

It must have been a matter of minutes, but to Piya it seemed like an eternity. To have a wet towel over her head, groping in the dark, not knowing what awaited her at the next step. He walked ahead of her most of the way. The stairway down was the most dangerous. There was not a soul on the stairs, and there was no telling if a terrorist would appear in front of them and gun them down at any moment. When they reached the ground floor, they could hear movement and cries down the corridor. Both of them huddled behind the door, not wanting to open it and face a terrorist, and willing it to not open from the other side either. After some minutes though, He risked opening the door. He craned his neck to see if there was anyone on that side. The corridor was deserted, and both of them ran for the exit.

A blast of fresh air hit Piya's face as she exited the hotel. There were police cars parked all around the exit. Immediately, He raised His arms, indicating that He was unarmed and she followed suit. A voice on a mobile loudspeaker asked them to come up ahead slowly. Those steps were the longest in Piya's life, with the most inane things filling her head. *I hope they don't shoot us now, thinking we are terrorists. I need to get home. My dress feels sticky. I need a shower. I think I lost my purse. And my Jimmy Choos. I haven't eaten in so long.* A police officer came up to them and asked them to come with him. They were taken to a police van and asked some questions—Where were they? What did they see? How did they come out? Was there anyone in the corridors? Did they see any terrorists? Did they get a sense of how many terrorists there were?

Piya's mind had clamped up. He did most of the talking. All she could think of was tea. She asked one of the police officers if she could have tea. The police officer had none to give her. She called Ayesha, who was waiting near the cordon behind the hotel. A police officer accompanied them to the back of the hotel. She held on to Him, but he was unresponsive and quiet. He said abruptly, 'I will speak to you later Piya. I'm going to leave.'

'Where will you go? Go home with Ayesha. She is waiting here.'

'I don't want to see anyone right now Piya, much less make conversation with anyone.'

'I am barefoot,' was all she could think of saying.

He squeezed her hand and said, 'You will be home soon. You'll be fine, don't worry.'

Piya hugged Him once more and smelled Him, with the mingled smells of smoke and dampness. He smiled as she walked away from Him and looked back to see Him once more.

That was the last time she ever saw Him.

Ayesha and Anand were waiting by a police van for her. The look on Anand's face told her everything she wanted to know. He hugged her and gave her some tea from the flask they had carried from home. Piya's heart broke on seeing him. How difficult it must be for him, to know that his wife was in danger at the Taj and was with her lover. She did not know how to react, what to say to him. Piya rode home in silence...thinking about Him, thinking of what she would tell Anand. But Anand didn't ask her anything. Not that day, not ever. It was a taboo between them. Anand began to travel more for work. He was hardly home, preferring to remain silent on something that could rip their family apart. He was polite and distant with her, and it had been months since he had moved to hold her or to make love to her.

The day after the Taj, He walked out of her life. And threw her out of His heart. He refused to meet her and after a few calls, refused to speak to her again.

Piya flinched as she drank water, watching people milling about her. How she clung and clung to Him. The more He distanced himself, the more she had clung on. Crying, fighting, cajoling, wheedling, lying, begging—everything she could do to not make Him leave her, to make him stay.

Her heart constricted with incredible pain.

He told her He was over her. And He did not want to have anything to do with her any longer. Piya could not figure it out. She fought hard for Him. She fought Him the most for letting Himself stay with her.

Piya wondered how that night at the Taj had changed them both in such different ways. She felt closer to Him after the trauma they had gone through together. She felt grateful that they had escaped unscathed. For her, it was a sign that they were meant to be together. That there was no immorality in their being together. They had been protected by a higher power. After that night, He had become cold, distant, and then nasty and harsh with her. She had tried talking to Him, but His voice reflected irritation, indifference, impatience, until her heart broke into a million small pieces.

Grief and letting go of a relationship indeed have many stages, Piya thought as she played with her wedding ring on the Bandstand bench. When He had begun to distance himself, she was beside herself with shock. Disbelieving. He, who had been so tender with her, was telling her He did not care anymore? It could not be happening to them, to her. Then came anger—when she blasted Him. Nastily ticked Him off. And all the while, her heart hurt. Hurt with pain and anger that He had suddenly changed so much and she looked so needy. There were days when she could not get out of bed. She would lie down, head under her pillow, thinking, going over all the events of those few weeks to try and understand what went wrong. Perhaps she was unlovable. Maybe when He got to know her better He realized she really wasn't all that good. Maybe He did not find her interesting anymore.

The sea at Bandstand was a roiling mucky brown and the heavy monsoon clouds loomed menacingly overhead. Most of the walkers and runners were out with umbrellas or raincoats. The air was redolent with the smell of corn being roasted. Families milled around eating corn, taking pictures in the Walk of Fame. Piya looked at their faces, the happiness of an evening out together, of couples in sync with each other, and wondered where she had lost it. She saw children skipping about their parents and marveled at their happiness. There were days when the noise of her sorrow was so loud in her head that she couldn't understand what her children were saying. Anand's silence killed her, but she had no courage to bring up the topic. She had no way of telling him that she needed him the most now. To be hugged and told she was worthy. To be consoled that she was lovable. That she mattered. What could she say to Anand anyway? She had crossed a line; she had cheated on her husband. How could she tell him that she had cheated because she had fallen in love with Him? And now struggled with her feelings?

How could someone who had touched her but a few times, come to dictate her life so much? That all her time became BH and AH— Before Him and After Him.

People talk of happiness. Of how it feels against your tongue, against your skin. How it makes you feel, in your blood and in your heart. How it warms you up like the sun. How it smells like a warm, safe cookie. How it sits like a cloak that is multicolored and multi-faceted, how it reflects hope. And life.

And Piya wondered if anyone had described sadness. Sadness came in so many different ways to her. It could make her feel gray and dull on a perfectly sunny day. It would make her shiver in the damp of the Mumbai rains. It was like a leech that slowly sucked out life from her body. It was like lead in her body that pulled her toward the ground. It was the dull ache in her bones. It was the cloak that smothered all other emotions. Some days, she could not understand what her children were chattering about. Their words and sounds were undecipherable for her. Sadness was old Bollywood melodies, old movies of betrayal and loss. It made her want to forget, made her want to eat sleeping pills every night so that her fatigued mind would stop thinking. It made her want to remember, so that she would not fall asleep. It made her want to pace up and down. It made her want to sit down because there was no energy in her legs. It made her old. It made her not want to look into the mirror anymore because she saw failure there.

Piya's steps never took her back to that little place on Pali Hill that they had discovered together. One day, she saw some trucks lined up in the narrow lane, and understood that it was all over. The place had finally been discovered by the land sharks. And her special place, from a special time in her life, had also been taken away.

As she sat on that Bandstand bench, Piya yearned for a simpler time, a time when she was only a married woman—happy, or at least not terribly unhappy, with what she had in life. For the time when she was not a scarlet woman. She yearned for her lost innocence. She yearned for the stupid, mundane thoughts that used to crowd her mind—maids, kids, work, colleagues and their petty concerns and stupid misunderstandings.

Anything to help her forget. To forget the nastiness she faced when

He did not want her in His life any longer. The horror of being called names, of being accused of being a slut, a home-breaker, a blackmailer. Of being told that He pitied her because he was over her, and she was still stuck in the moment. Of being told she was pathetic because could she not see, He did not care? The shame of it all.

The monsoon clouds broke over her head and Piya's tears also broke free.

She dreamt of Him still—of Him holding her, kissing her, touching her. Of His hands. Of His smile. She thought most often about His eyes. His eyes that had made her want Him when she was younger, and the very same eyes that made her feel loved, wanted, desired, and sexy. She yearned for that one call, one SMS to tell her He thought of her, that He cared. But there was only deafening silence. When He had wanted her, nothing would stop Him. And when He did not want her anymore, nothing could keep Him with her.

The only person she could unburden herself with was Ayesha. Ayesha felt her pain and tried to make her feel better.

—Maybe he got shaken by the Taj episode Piya. People react with fight or flight instincts at times of crisis. He chose flight.

—But could He have forgotten me so soon?

—Men compartmentalize things. Once he was done with you, he shut that part off.

—Feels good to know I was so easy to compartmentalize. And be shut out with such ease.

—You misunderstand me Piya. He may think of you, he is only human. But he has reckoned that in the scheme of things, the relationship with you is not worth the consequences, babe. Look at what he would lose—his kids, his wife, the life he has built. Forget him, assess what you would lose in carrying on with this relationship. Anand would definitely leave you. Then what would you be left with? And do you really want to gift your kids a broken home?

—Maybe you're right. But I wish He had not left me like this. Had given me time to adapt to His changed heart.

—I know you don't see it right now, but he has done you a favor.

Piya knew Ayesha was right, but at the moment the grief of losing Him was too much. As was the anger, the hurt, and the feeling of being used and discarded.

Piya got back home from her run and opened her laptop. She logged on to Facebook to see Him. That was the only place she still could; she often wondered why He had not yet blocked her from it, when He had blocked her from every other place in his life. There was fresh activity on His page. He had gone for a holiday with His family and there were pictures of them all. She skimmed through the pictures until she came upon one with Him and His younger son. Piya sat looking at that picture for a long time. He was holding His son who was trying to wiggle out of His bear hug. The smile of delight, of innocence, of a secure childhood hit Piya like a brick. *Who would ever want to break that heart and take that smile off the young one's face? Can I really blame Him for leaving me?*

No, she thought. That was never the intention anyway. What kills me is that He lied, simply to get me where He wanted me, and then threw me out of His life.

Perhaps forgiveness would come, creep up on her, a little every day. Maybe forgiveness meant that He was not the first thing she thought of in the morning. Or was not reminded of Him when she heard the *koyal* sing outside her window. Or did not want to call Him when something significant happened to her. Or when she stopped looking over her shoulder because she could not feel His presence anymore. Or when she managed to win Anand's trust back. She would be able to forgive Him when she could feel the world around her once again. And forgive herself. And trust herself again.

Piya's finger hovered over the 'unfriend' button. She hesitated. This meant that she would never see Him again. And that she was letting Him go.

Piya looked at the father-son picture once She moved her index finger on His face and let it linger on his lips for a moment. She pressed the 'unfriend' button and then, on her privacy settings, blocked him from her FB. She breathed easy. It was time to stop unraveling, and time to start living again.

Veera

When I conceived after 14 years of emotional torture, I knew instinctively that this child was going to survive. Almost five years before KD was born, *maaji* had totally given up on me and my womb. Thankfully it meant that I no longer had to go to *sadhus* of all kinds, and be forced to eat herbal *bootis* to conceive. Of course she would lament to everyone about her misfortune—to the members of her *satsang*, to her friends, to her relatives, to the in-laws of my sisters-in-law, to the help at home, the shopkeepers, the auto guys, and strangers too. Everyone who would lend her half an ear.

But this baby in my womb gave me hope. Somehow I knew my life was about to change. I mustered up the courage to tell Gurujitji to ensure that *maaji* did not throw out the household help this time. I lied to him and told him that I felt sick all the time, and the doctor had ordered me to take bed rest. The doctor was a kind lady. She had witnessed *maaji's* behavior with me for years, and I pleaded with her to corroborate my story. The next time I had to visit the doctor, I told Gurujitji that she wanted him to come with me. *Maaji* was livid and told him that men did not go for such things. But he decided to come with me anyway and the doctor asked him to ensure that I got my rest.

I had no idea if I was carrying a boy or a girl. But I prayed to the Guru Granth Sahib every day. I wanted a child. A healthy child. Preferably a male child. But I would be grateful for whatever Babaji gave me, as long as it lived.

When finally my baby was born, I held that bundle in my hands and nuzzled into his baby skin; I knew I had found home. I knew this child of mine would live. When he opened his eyes the first time and looked at me, even though he could not possibly see me clearly, I fell in love. I knew this love would last forever. That was my Kuldeep.

Look at me. It has been years since I called KD by his real name— Kuldeep. That is what he was—the light that would take the name of our family ahead. Kuldeep began to be called KD in college and slowly all of us got used to calling him KD too.

Namita and Piya don't understand why I love KD so much. I don't love him so much only because he is a boy. That is one reason, of course. If after so many troubles I had had a girl child first, *maaji* would have made life miserable for me. The real reason is the change in my life. After years, I was happy. I got more confidence to demand things. I was not looked upon as a *baanj* anymore. People started looking at me more indulgently. Suddenly, I was not a pariah.

I was a changed woman. I looked different too. In the mirror, I saw a young woman, glowing and happy. No matter what *maaji* did to make my life miserable, I was determined that my child would have a good life. I stole money from her to buy milk and fruits, and even candy that my KD wanted. I hankered after Veerji for clothes for the baby and money instead of mangoes. I made Gurujitji buy me a pram for KD and every evening, I would take my baby out.

Gurujitji doted on KD. He would take him from me after his morning feed and walk outside with him. He was always speaking to KD—showing him leaves on the trees or birds. Father and son would sometimes sit on the stairs of the apartment block and watch people go by, or dogs get into fights. Gurujitji's attitude changed towards me as well. He did not say anything in front of *maaji*, but he started giving me money once his salary went up. He bought me a sari and told *maaji* that his boss's wife had sent it for me. On weekends, he would accompany me when I took KD for a walk.

You may not appreciate what it all meant to me. The fact that after 15 long years, I finally mustered the courage to tell Gurujitji that I wanted to go to Delhi to meet my parents. I knew there was no way *maaji* could throw me out of the house now. I still remember the pride with which I held my bundle of joy when I disembarked at the Delhi station. And the joy of seeing my parents and the quiet satisfaction that the worst was over for me. Veerji had tears in his eyes, and in his eyes I saw regret and remorse that he did not fight harder for me. I never blamed him. He did the best he could for me and I loved him dearly. He had been the one that kept me going in those bleak years. After the bitter winter that had lasted for so long for me, I was finally happy. And I would make the most of my summer.

From Chimbai Lane where we lived, it was an easy stroll to Bandra's Bandstand. Mind you, it was not the same as it looks now. It is all concrete now, with a stupid Walk of Fame where famous filmstars have their hand imprints. If these illustrious people had died before someone conceived of this stupidity, their names, instead of their hand imprints, are on one of the spaces. What is the point, I wonder? Of making something like this in a busy place where all the people like to come, sit around, and walk. And a guard stationed there protects these precious hands with a stick in his hand. When I go for a walk in the evenings, I am almost tempted to hit him with my stick.

Bandstand in the late 1960s and early 1970s was not so well organized. But there was a walkway and in the evenings, just like today, loads of people came out to walk. Maids and young mothers with babies in strollers, old people sitting together or walking while they chat. And lovers everywhere. In a city that offers no space, these lovers would walk to the edge of the stones to grab some private time. *Bhel puri* and *sev puri* vendors and *chaiwallahs* and *pepsicolawallahs*—with those narrow little tubes made of plastic filled tightly with flavored ice—would wander around. I would walk KD and then sit near a bench on the side of the Sea Rock Hotel. It was a good vantage point. I would watch stylishly dressed people go into the hotel. I never mustered enough courage to enter it though. How could I? I did not belong. My clothes were neat, but old and faded. Even though I scrubbed my face, wore *kajal*, and looked presentable, I did not look rich, or even like someone who could afford a cup of tea there. The guard at the entry would most certainly turn me away.

But I used to love to sit there and watch the people on Bandstand. See the way they dressed, talked, interacted with each other. Sometimes, if I had a little money I would buy *bhel puri* or *chana jor* and sit and relish it. This was my quiet time. A breather in a busy day. I would relax and watch KD. Watch him look at people. Watch him smile, gesticulate, make funny faces. It was my happiest time in the day.

It was many days before I noticed the young man and his girlfriend. I noticed him because of his thick curly hair. They would always sit together. She would be reading a book, and the boy was busy with his sketch pad. One day I saw him watching me closely. I almost choked on my *bhel puri* and felt blood rush to my face. I quickly turned my face away, and kept it turned the other way. I debated if I should get up and walk away, and then didn't, because I did not want him to see he affected me. More importantly, I did not want to lose my evening pleasure.

The next morning, I was nervous the entire day about seeing him again when I went to Bandstand in the evening. But that evening, he wasn't on the bench. I heaved a sigh of relief, and after a few days, when I didn't see him again, I stopped looking in the direction of the bench to check if he had come.

One evening, as I was feeding KD a banana, I felt someone come and sit next to me. I smiled as I looked up and my smile froze. It was that sketch guy. He smiled back at me. I felt my face flush again and turned my attention back to KD.

—How old is he?

—Nine months.

—He is very good-looking. Takes after you?

I kept quiet.

—I am not flirting. Please don't mind. I have been watching you for many days. And sketched you without permission. Would you like to see?

I looked at him sharply. He raised an eyebrow.

—You make a very pretty sight with your child. When you look at the sun over the sea, your face looks lovely. I like the way your face lights up when you are observing people.

I did not know whether to be offended or flattered. To be angry or happy. To talk or not. I sort of muttered and asked to see the sketch. The boy was talented. And his sketch book was full of drawings of KD and me, or of me alone. Me feeding KD, and his big innocent eyes watching me with love. Me looking out at the sunset. Me watching people. Me counting my money.

How had I not seen him sketch me for so long? He must have been observing me forever. I asked him as much. He said, 'I have been drawing you for about a month. And before that I was observing you.'

'That is not very nice,' I said. 'Why would you pick on me out of all the people in Bandstand?'

He smiled and said, 'You seem to be the only one who does not have a friend here. And I notice how you look at people but never meet their eye, almost as if you don't want anyone to approach you.'

He spoke as if he knew me. 'I enjoy my peace here. This is the time of the day I get to spend alone with Kuldeep.'

He said, 'Before we continue talking, let me tell you my name at least. I am Ravi. And you don't have to tell me your name. I call you the lady in the sari.'

I laughed. 'So what would you call me if I wore a suit tommorow?'

—Suit*wali*.

—Or if I wore a dress the next day?

—Dress*wali*.

It was so easy to laugh with him. His eyes would crinkle up with mirth and we would laugh and laugh. At stupid things like KD trying to catch a bubble. At somebody eagerly biting into their corn on the cob and singeing their mouth. At the way the guard would shoo away the love birds.

I met Sangeeta too. She and Ravi were old friends, and she would join him whenever she could at Bandstand. She was studying at NM College. Nice girl she was. In love with him I felt. He was nice and gentle with her. Ravi was that kind of a person—compassionate and funny.

He could make you feel like you were the most important person in the world for him. He would be a good catch for Sangeeta. When I got to know Ravi better, I asked him if he was in love with Sangeeta. He looked at me, 'Would I not tell you if I was? Don't you know me better?'

Life is indeed in the little moments. I hear people say it all the time, 'Don't think about the small things, they are not important.' I say, don't forget any of the small things. Life exists in those. Life for me was in KD. In the way his face puckered up the first time he tasted *kairi*. Or the way his lower lip trembled when he held a balloon and it burst in front of his face. Life happened to me when I would wait for Ravi to come down from his apartment on Bandstand. It was a pleasure to watch him sketch. The concentration on his face, and the way a lock of his hair fell over his forehead as he worked. The way his hands and lips moved in tandem when he was telling a story. It was in that simple feeling of wanting to put that curly lock of hair away.

I began to look forward to our evenings together. Ravi was a rich boy from Delhi. He was deeply interested in art, and his father had given him a year to indulge his passion. After that he would have to join the family business. He was almost the same age as me, 27. He had had a happy childhood and had never known deprivation—thank God. I never shared with him what happened with me at home. In that space in Bandstand, those problems did not exist. I refused to mar my happiness in the brief moments that I had there. Ravi was part of that landscape. Someone I met, spent some time with, and came back refreshed.

Had anyone paid me attention at home, they would have seen the change in me. But *maaji* only saw the things I did not do right, and Gurujitji had never noticed me anyway. I started dressing better, even though I had few clothes. I would leave my hair in a ponytail sometimes, or tie it up in a loose braid, or even make a stylish bun. I started wearing a light lipstick. In the mirror, I began to seem a happy young woman again.

What I do know is that Ravi brought me happiness. I used to look forward to meeting him every evening, and I used to enjoy the time we spent together. I think there must not be a single person whose life we had not dissected together. We would sit together making up stories about anyone who caught our fancy. That old woman seemed like she gave her daughter-in-law a hard time, because the daughter-in-law would ignore her after settling her down on a bench. That man's girlfriend must have left him as every evening he would sit down glumly while he ate peanuts. And what is that old man telling the young girl? A lewd joke perhaps! We used to think that the old men were the worst of the lot—frustrated, desperate, and hitting on women of all shapes, sizes and colors.

Ravi once took me to the big hotel on Bandstand for *chai*. I was so nervous. I kept smoothing down my sari and tucking in my hair. Ravi smiled at me. 'Don't be nervous. Behave as if you do this every day.'

'But my sari looks so old,' I complained.

Ravi linked his arm in mine and said, 'Do you know who owns most of the money in Bombay? The Parsis and the Gujaratis. And do you know how to identify the richest among them? The ones who wear the cheapest clothes, as if they couldn't be bothered. It's all in the attitude, remember that.'

Years later, when I had enough money to socialize with the city's rich, I thought of what Ravi had said. KD's lawyer is one of the top lawyers of Mumbai, a nice lady. And she told me she never wears suits that are more than five hundred rupees apiece! It really is in the attitude.

Ravi stayed in a rented apartment in Bandstand. The first time I went there was because I had accidentally dropped tea on KD and he was distraught. Ravi insisted that I go up to his apartment and clean up KD. To my lower-middle-class eyes, the apartment looked so big and elegant. It smelled of wealth. I was uncomfortable, but not for long. Ravi had that quality of making me feel like I belonged. Like nothing was amiss. That we were only two friends meeting at his place over a cup of tea.

I went to his place many times over the next six months. KD loved crawling there. We would sip tea and watch the sun go down. From our higher vantage point we would look at people on Bandstand and continue weaving stories about them.

Once Ravi happened to mention that he missed home-cooked meals, *aloo paranthas* most of all, because his cook did not make them the way they are made in Delhi. Thick with spicy potato filling. So whenever *maaji* was not home, I began to cook something for Ravi—*aloo paranthas, chhole, rajma, pulao*. I would put the box with the food at the bottom of the bag I carried for KD on our evening walks. It gave me much happiness to watch Ravi eat. He ate with such relish and love.

Ravi is the one who made me aware that I was a good cook. In all the years that I had cooked for my family, no one had ever told me that. When Ravi first told me that I cooked very well, I laughed it off. *A young lonely boy deprived of home-cooked meals*, I thought. Then Ravi started planning what I could do with my cooking. I could start a *dabba* service, help other caterers, or start a restaurant. I had to constantly remind him that this was me he was talking about—a young, uneducated mother, with no resources!

After all these years, some smells still remind me of Ravi. The sharp smell of the Bandstand sea—filled with the muck of Mumbai. The smell of corn in the monsoon rain. The smell of cutting *chai* with ginger and over-brewed tea leaves. These are happy smells for me. Smells that linger and bring memories of warmth and love.

Then I got pregnant with Namita and could not step out of the house for almost three months. I had severe morning sickness, and I could not retain any food or liquid in those months. I was so sick that Gurujitji insisted that *maaji* hire a full-time maid to take care of KD.

He would come back early and take KD out for a walk. Sangeeta came to visit me once. I gave her a letter for Ravi. She said she would give it to him.

I was so restless in those days. I wanted to escape the house and meet Ravi. I wanted to tell him what had happened. I could not. And when I did get to Bandstand after four months, Ravi was gone. I went to his apartment, and the building guard told me that Ravi had moved back to Delhi.

I never met Sangeeta either.

There was nothing I could do.

Namita

To: Piyar@gmail.com
From: namitap@gmail.com
Jun 28, 2013
8 p.m.

How is Mom doing? And how long do the doctors think she will be like this? I think of her all the time when we are shooting. It upsets me, makes me guilty, as if I am not being a good daughter....

I can't remember Mom being loving towards me...not once. And that hurts. I remember only pain. Like the time she finally realized what I was up to.

I was near Dalal Street that day when the bombs went off at Bombay Stock Exchange in 1993. I was working on a photography shoot for Maharashtra Tourism. That day, we were to photograph the BSE and all the buzz around it. It was the 12th of March, I remember. I had been in front of BSE since 6.30 in the morning. It was a beautiful morning. Still not too hot or humid. As I checked the lighting and various positions for shots, I noticed how the street filled up with vendors and their little service boys on the roadside. They set up stalls or tables with newspapers, fixed deposit papers, official documents of listed companies, pens, paper and other stationery, and food and drinks. I noted absently how enterprising people in Mumbai were—to provide small relevant services to consumers. I made a mental note of the food I would eat after the shoot was over. I had already wolfed down a steaming hot *vada pav* with cutting *chai*, and even taken some pictures of the *vada pav* guy and his small assistant boy. That boy, no more than 12, I think, was so excited to be photographed. I had planned my post-shoot meal too. I would eat *idli* and *vada* dunked in *sambar*. (Remember how cheap we used to be—asking for the stuff to be soaked in *sambar* because we figured we got more *sambar* that way!)

Soon the roads were clogged with buses, taxis, cars, cycles, people; it's the kind of madness that defines Mumbai. I was delighted. I had planned a shot of the BSE building with loads of activity in front of it. BSE was a symbol of Mumbai—the financial capital of India. Its people, and the buzz and energy that make Mumbai; I was going to capture all that. By the time the shoot was over it was one in the afternoon already. My team and I headed to the nearest *Udipi* joint for our *idli-vada-sambar*.

It had become really hot, and I had a splitting headache by then. My hair clung to my face and neck, and my clothes were stuck to me like second skin. I wanted to wrap up and go home and take a cold shower. I must have been stinking of sweat, and more sweat.

When the first bombs went off, I thought there had been a massive accident. The noise was unbelievable. And then people started to scream, and all at once there was mayhem on the road. Even before I could process what had gone wrong, I started running towards the noise—in the opposite direction from everyone else, because they were running away from it. As I ran, I took pictures. I did not allow myself to think that the scene in front of me was gory. Parts of BSE looked bombed out, there were dead bodies, limbs scattered all around. There were wounded people who were screaming horribly and some good Samaritans who were trying to help them. The *vada pav* joint that we had eaten at was no longer there, and I wondered where the little boy was, the one who had served us that morning.

Much later in the day, the enormity of what had happened began to sink in. This was one of the 13 bombs that ripped Mumbai apart that day. None of this penetrated my consciousness at that time. All I knew was that I had recorded part of this history. In the office, as I developed the pictures, the story unfolded before my eyes. I went numb. The pictures captured the brutality, the loss, the pain, and misery quite well. Abhishek was impressed and without telling me, he sent some of my pictures in a photography contest organized by a leading magazine the following month. When I walked into office several months later, there was celebration because I had won the contest. The magazine also wanted to showcase all my pictures of that fateful day at the venue for the awards ceremony.

I wanted Mom and Dad to come and see what I had achieved. To understand that I was good at this and to let me choose photography as a career. So I told them I had got passes for a photography awards ceremony and wanted to take them.

There can be the best day in your life. And there can be the worst day of your life. For me, that was the day. Dad was delighted at the surprise and so proud of me. He met all the folks I worked with with such affection. Mom, on the other hand, sulked throughout. Her face was set in a grimace and she refused to talk to anyone. Not once, Piya, not once did she tell me I had done well, or that she was proud of me. See the picture of me with my award and Mom and Dad. She has such a grimace in that too. As a mother, could she not have been happy for me that day? Even if I had not told her about my photography, couldn't she get past the fact that I had hidden this passion of mine from her?

Did she have to embarrass me so much in front of the people who mattered to me?

You may not understand it Piya, but when a child does not get her mother's love and approval, she has a streak of insecurity all her life. And I think that is the reason I went downhill when it came to my personal life. I seeked and seeked love, not understanding that I came across as so needy and desperate that I never managed to have a fulfilling relationship. I never thought I was good enough, so people would never love me if I showed them my true self. How could they love me, when my own mother did not?

To: Piyar@gmail.com
From: namitap@gmail.com
Jun 29, 2013
1 a.m.

What do you think Mom's reaction would be if she knew the number of men I have slept with? According to her, I am the black sheep of the family and am already living in sin with Atul! LOL
Piya darling. It is actually really cool to be a single woman in Mumbai. You can drink in the bar with your friends, take an auto back at three at night, or even walk back home on Pali Hill at night, and no one will trouble you. Your neighbors don't think that the reason you come back late at night is because you were out selling your body. You can wear the clothes you like and most men do not think you are flaunting your assets to turn them on.
And you can get men, who are looking for a good time—no strings attached. I like such men who are obvious about their lust and don't mix it with love. Lust is so much more uncomplicated than love. You want someone, you get them. There is no need for an elaborate mating ritual, of doing the whole song and dance about how much you love the person, can't live without them. The truth is, your body is responding sexually, physically, to someone else's, and you find a way to fulfill that sexual desire in a mutually satisfying way. The episode may lead to something deeper, or it may not.
What is this whole thing about sex anyway? If Indians were to be quizzed in public, they would flat out deny having sex at all. And what, most of their children were born by Immaculate Conception? Women will deny having pre-marital sex, and guys will inflate their experiences and try to sound more experienced than they really are. Because sex is such a taboo, there is such a thrill in it. In dark, dingy corners of a cinema hall, on the sandy corners of Juhu beach, on benches in parks under the *dupatta*, in little-known corners of

colleges, in sleazy hotels that let you rent rooms on hourly basis, fumbling and sex is happening all the time. Just like there is extra-marital sex everywhere.

But let's just say this—if I don't see it, it does not exist!

I may have a little black diary of my own, but that does not make me loose or slutty. My mantra: If men can do it, so can I. And I don't care about people who judge me.

There are four kinds of men I have met.

Type 1: They are fascinated with me. When they see me, they see this curly-haired, sharp-talking, abrasive woman who plays hard to get. To them it becomes a challenge to get me into bed. These are the ones who play the game of love. And their pillow talk reveals to me all I could ever know about their wives, families, work and their world.

Type 2: The under-confident beings who cannot believe their good fortune that I have paid them attention. They blossom under my attention and will come into my bed with a ring in their pockets. I would never accept a proposal from Type 2—I can't spend my life pampering a guy and boosting his ego and morale.

Type 3: The hot model bodies that are super-self-obsessed. I love these guys in bed. They are full of themselves and want to perform really well so they live up to their macho reputations. They hope you will spread the good word around. They are charming in their own way—not marriage material, but great fun.

Type 4: The guy who will hit on anything and try his luck. My girl-friends respect boundaries more than some men I know. We don't hit on men our girlfriends are crushing on, or are in a relationship with. But some men I know will try their luck, even if they are dating your best friend (and in some cases, also married to them). Sang's guy asked me if I would kiss him when she got out of the car. Really? What an asshole!

Two kinds of men I don't do:

1. Men who lie to get you into their bed. Who spin yarns of love they feel for you. They screw up my mind. Get honest guys, and learn the four-letter word—LUST.

2. Colleagues: too complicated, messy, and a bit incestuous.

To: namitap@gmail.com
From: Piyar@gmail.com
June 30, 2013
11 a.m.

I like the way you have classified your men. What would make you sleep with a Type 2 anyway? Or, for that matter, Type 1s, especially if they are married. Oh okay…don't bother answering that. I know what you will say—that you are not married to their wives, and did not take the sacred vows of fidelity. And that you don't sleep with the husbands/boyfriends of your girl friends. I know you sis! I admire you Namita. You do keep the creepy ones at bay.

I envy you. I have only two men I can talk about. I was so dumb that I did not even have a boyfriend in college. Where did I have the time? I was working with Mom when I was in college.

You are no slut. You are not committed to anyone in a long-term relationship so you are not cheating on anyone. I am the slut. What I did was unpardonable.

To: Piyar@gmail.com
From: namitap@gmail.com
Jun 30, 2013
10.12 p.m.

Oh please, cut yourself some slack Piya. Fuck HIM. He was an asshole. You made a mistake. All of us do. He is the kind of guy I would NEVER do. Cowards who don't have the courage to speak their mind, and disappear at the first sign of trouble.

And by the way, little one, perhaps it is not so bad after all. You were always the shy and quiet one. Too scared to do anything. In a way I think the experience did you good. At least you did something out of the box!!! For however brief a time, you were deliriously happy and felt love. Sometimes that is enough Piya. Very few people can feel love this intensely. So say a small prayer for you, for him, and move on. You are too beautiful for crap like him to disturb you for so long.

To: namitap@gmail.com
From: Piyar@gmail.com
Jun 30, 2013
11.15 p.m.

And you made me smile!

To: Piyar@gmail.com
From: namitap@gmail.com
Jun 30, 2013
11.18 p.m.

Who knows, 'he' might be a little like our super brother KD!

To: namitap@gmail.com
From: Piyar@gmail.com
Jun 30, 2013
11.21 p.m.

OMG, you know about KD? I thought I was the only one who suspected it.

To: Piyar@gmail.com
From: namitap@gmail.com
Jun 30, 2013
11.30 p.m.

Of course I know about our illustrious brother. I wonder what Mom would say if she knew? Or if she does really know this about him? When he got married, Deepa's husband sent Mana a note. Deepa was really distraught about KD's marriage, and had been trying to speak to him. When he did not speak to her, she overdosed on sleeping pills and spilled the beans to her husband. He was furious. What could he have said to KD anyway? So he sent that note. KD did not even go and meet Deepa again. How humiliating for her!

To: namitap@gmail.com
From: Piyar@gmail.com
Jul 1, 2013
00.21 a.m.

Sorry, had to get Mom cleaned up. Oh dear. Was it that Deepa from his gym? The pretty young thing? I saw them both outside the gym once, before he got married.
Poor Deepa.
And poor Mana.

To: Piyar@gmail.com
From: namitap@gmail.com
Jul 1, 2013
00.51 a.m.

Yes, the very same Deepa. Dumb of her, I think, to take those pills. And then to tell her husband. What did she expect? That KD would have married her? KD would have married only the girl Mom picked for him. You know how he is.
I used to feel bad for Mana, but I don't feel bad anymore. If she chooses to turn a blind eye to what KD does, it is her problem. It's her choice.
Btw, I am meeting someone in Mumbai next month. I met him on-line about two months ago and we have been chatting ever since.

To: namitap@gmail.com
From: Piyar@gmail.com
Jul 1, 2013
1.30 a.m.

WHAT? Who is this? Some friend of yours?

To: Piyar@gmail.com
From: namitap@gmail.com
Jul 1, 2013
1.40 a.m.

Just a guy I used to know a long time ago in college. He had a big crush on me and I had a massive one on him too. He is in South Africa now, and is coming to India to meet me.

To: namitap@gmail.com
From: Piyar@gmail.com
Jul 1, 2013
2 a.m.

Huh? Is he married? And what can you say to someone you have not met in decades?

To: Piyar@gmail.com
From: namitap@gmail.com
Jul 1, 2013
2.05 a.m.

LOL. Not only have I not met him, I had not even thought of him these past decades. When he sent me a friend request on Facebook, it took me a while to figure out who it was. But something clicked Piya. I remembered things I had forgotten and how much I had liked him in the past. Even the fact that I never spoke to him again because he asked to kiss me!
And what began innocuously enough has grown into something so much bigger.
You may remember him. Rahul Jain.

To: namitap@gmail.com
From: Piyar@gmail.com
Jul 1, 2013
2.20 a.m.

OMG, of course I remember him. Good-looking dude he was. You had such a massive crush on him. I remember your notebooks filled with his name and yours. You would cross his name and yours with that silly game of love, like, hate, adore. So is he married? Kids?

To: Piyar@gmail.com
From: namitap@gmail.com
Jul 1, 2013
2.25 a.m.

He's divorced. And Piya, he remembers everything about you all. I had forgotten that he had a brother, even his nickname. Now I seem to remember everything and I am constantly thinking of him!!

To: namitap@gmail.com
From: Piyar@gmail.com
Jul 1, 2013
2.40 a.m.

Perfect then, Namita. Maybe he is the guy you have been waiting for all your life! Yay!

To: Piyar@gmail.com
From: namitap@gmail.com
Jul 1, 2013
2.45 a.m.

I don't know that Piya. I love him. I feel very strongly about him, and we have not even met yet! What if we meet and it is not the same? He may have body odor. Or a voice that does not sound as good in person…. What if he does not like me?
Also, I wonder if these feelings are for real. I mean, I have only spoken to him on phone, and we write to each other all the time. But what if this is not who he is? Maybe he says all the right things because he knows that is what I want to hear. I wonder at my foolishness too. Can you fall in love 'virtually'?

To: namitap@gmail.com
From: Piyar@gmail.com
Jul 1, 2013
3.10 a.m.

Thank god I am in the hospital tonight, else, I would have been fast asleep at home and not had this exciting conversation with you!

Namita, what is wrong in falling in love virtually? You knew this person, even if it was for a brief period of your life. So for one, he is not a stranger.

Second, is this not true for every arranged marriage in India? Or even a love match? You present the best of yourself, and hope that the other person will be intrigued and excited enough to commit him/herself to you. Unraveling happens when you get married!

At least you know what he looks like, and something more about him! What did I know of Anand when I married him? I met him at a friend's party in Bangkok and enjoyed his company for an evening. When I came back to India, his parents came over with the proposal! I have come to believe that marriages are destined. You will meet that one person out of several billion people in this world, and somehow it will click, and somehow you will get married. And hope for happiness later!!

And who can NOT love you? You are a rockstar my sister.

Gudia

It was always so embarrassing. To ask Piya madam for money. I had to think of new excuses every time. Sometimes it was for the leaky roof in my one-room house, or for my parents in the village who needed money to buy seeds for the new crop. I have asked for money for my son's fee, for a cycle for my daughter, even an advance on the pretext that my injured husband had not gone to work for a month.

All lies, of course. If I couldn't convince her, make her feel sorry for me, then a brutal beating awaited me at home. Lies that I am certain she saw through, but gave me the money anyway. I don't have the courage to tell her that my no-good husband Raja forces me to demand more money from her. Compared to other *memsahibs*, Piya madam is very generous—she gives me all her old clothes, old utensils from the kitchen, leftovers from house parties, a bonus on Diwali and new clothes for the whole family, umbrellas and plastic *chappals* for the monsoons, and a shawl and blanket during winter.

Every time I protested, Raja's reaction was the same. His eyes would become wild and red. His fleshy face would contort with anger as he raged, 'She gives you used goods, and you are grateful for that? You take care of her household while she earns pots of gold from her business. For a simple meal of 10 rupees, she charges a hundred. Her driver tells me how much she shops. And how many dinners she goes to in fancy restaurants. What about the many holidays they go for abroad?'

—Yes Raja, but she pays me more than other maids get.

—She does you no favor. You are useful to her. The day you break a leg, or are very sick, she is not going to wait forever for you to come back to work. So make her pay.

I couldn't argue with him. I didn't like going to work with bruises on my body or face. I didn't fancy being beaten up in front of my children.

This time round, Raja wanted a new television. Those new ones with a flat screen. The smallest one would cost ₹21,000.

Sometimes the vast difference between Piya madam and us bothers me. I live in a small one-room *kholi* in the congested Khar Danda area. Full of chawls and small apartment buildings. I have to stand in line early in the morning to fill water from the community tap. Until a few years ago, we did not have a bathroom in our *kholi*. We had to stand in a queue to relieve ourselves in the stinking community toilets. The fishermen have large nets where they dry the fish. The whole area smells of urine, shit, putrid garbage, and drying fish. It makes me want to gag. There is no place for my children to play. I can't let my daughter go outside for long periods of time. Unemployed ruffians are always lurking around to feel up girls and take advantage of them.

Every morning, I wake up at four, stand in line for water, rush back home, cook, and pack tiffins for my children and Raja, make an afternoon snack for children when they came back from school and rush to be at Piya madam's house by eight. She has given me five saris, so I change into a fresh one when I enter her house. The first hour is madness, as I cook breakfast, and pack *dabbas* for madam and Anand sir. After I serve them breakfast, I get a breather for some time. I sit down with my sweetened *chai* and relax for half an hour. Then I begin my work again—cooking, cleaning the kitchen, supervising the children's maid and other staff. Piya madam trusts me, and she seldom raises her voice against me.

The change from my environment to Pali Hill is a drastic one. Piya madam's building is beautiful with lots of trees and a play area for children. Her house is a spacious three-bedroom apartment and always smells wonderful with flowers everywhere. When the other maids, especially Sheela, complain about the bathroom (servants have a separate one) or the fact that they have to wake up at seven with the children, I feel like slapping them. Sheela has forgotten where she comes from—a little village in Maharashtra, where her impoverished parents still live. I remember the time she joined work. A young girl of 13 who had never used a western toilet. Who did not even know how to brush her teeth. She was constantly hungry, and stuffed her mouth all the time. Sheela was so fascinated with all the things in the house that every week, when I surreptitiously checked her bags, I would find the girls' trinkets and baubles, dry fruits, even apples and bread. I reported all of this back to Piya madam, and she told Sheela sternly that if anything went missing in the house, she would be thrown out. I taught Sheela how to wash herself, to use the bathroom, and how to behave in a gentile house. And now she complains. Even though Piya madam lets her watch TV at night when the kids are asleep and her work is all done. Then again, I feel sorry for her. Which child would like to stay in someone else's house and work there?

I would not like such a life for my daughter. I want her to study well and get a job in a big company. I want her to get married to an educated man, and to not stay in a dirty place like Khar Danda.

Since I was a little girl, I have lived there. In a small one-room apartment with my parents. My mother worked as a *chutta bai*. She would sweep, mop, do the dishes, wash the clothes, and iron them. Ma worked in three houses and by the time she would come back, she used to be exhausted. I would fill a bucket with hot water, put salt in it, and make her dip her feet in it. Then I would make her a cup of tea and together we would sit and chat. She would tell me all the gossip in those houses and we used to marvel how rich people have so much money to buy useless things. Big fancy cars, televisions in every bedroom, sheets and towels that are changed every day, many dishes on the table for every meal, expensive foreign liquor, and lots of clothes and shoes. Our world, with its hand-to-mouth existence, was so different. Two-three pairs of hand-me-down clothes, *dal* and *chawal* when the months were good and *dal* and *roti* on days when there was not sufficient food for all of us. I used to eat fruit only when ma got some from the homes where she worked. I tore off empty pages from old notebooks she would get, and tied them with a thread to make my own notebook.

My father was a simple soul. He worked as a loader for a construction company. He was a loving father, till he started drinking. Then, he would thrash us on the slightest pretext. Ma always intervened to protect me from him and as a result she was beaten up the worst. In my anger I told her one day, 'I hate him. When I grow up, I will get us a house and I will throw him out.'

Ma stroked my head and said, 'It is not his fault, Gudia. He has a tough job. On top of that, his *seth* abuses him badly. It is not in the blood of a man to face so much humiliation.'

—So why does he take out his humiliation and frustration on us? Is he such a coward that he can't tell the *seth* anything?

—He is not a coward. It takes a different kind of courage to face that humiliation. I am sure he can beat up the *seth* too. But he has you to provide for. Where will we go if he does not earn? My salary is not enough.

Now, a mother myself, I understand what Ma meant. Raja works as a driver with a company. He gets a good salary, overtime, and a yearly bonus. Yet, the money is never enough. And Raja is greedy.

Always wanting more. He can't afford to lose his job, so he bullies me into asking Piya madam for money.

Sometimes I wonder what I saw in Raja. He has gray hair and has put on weight by drinking every night. He uses rough language, and does not hesitate to use his hand when he wants to prove he is right. Over the years, I think his face shows his bitterness with life. His constant ranting that life has not been good to him. If he had been born into a better family, he would have been rich.

Yet, he is not a bad guy. He still has his *yaar-dost* who he hangs out with, and who love him a lot. He is the life of all our functions. At Ganpati, he is devoted and organizes the *pandal* for Ganpati and His immersion in the sea too. He keeps out of trouble with the street gangs and has politely told the local politician that he will not do his illegal work or assist in raising funds for him.

Raja and I stayed in the same lane in Danda, and when we were younger, he was good-looking in a rugged sort of way. He would stand outside his doorway, dressed in fancy clothes, leaning against a motorcycle he owned. He would wear jeans, a bright polyester shirt, and there was always a cigarette on his lips. Whenever I crossed him and his group of friends, no one would whistle at me. Only Raja's eyes would follow me. AH! those feelings of young love. My heart used to beat wildly whenever I saw him, and I used to look forward to seeing him every day.

Then one day, Raja followed me to my cooking class. Ma did not want me to work in other people's homes. Cooks earned a lot more money and could do more than five houses in a day. It was more respectable to be a cook. So Ma arranged with one of the ladies in Khar who conducted cooking lessons for maids, and got me to join the classes. I used to love those classes. I learnt different kinds of cooking—Punjabi, Sindhi, south Indian, and Chinese. Now at Piya madam's house, I have learnt a lot more. She's taught me Thai, Continental, Kashmiri, Rajasthani, and Mughlai cooking like *seekh kababs, shammi kababs, tandoori* chicken, and different *biryanis.*

I knew Raja was behind me because he was softly humming a song.

I did not stop. I was so nervous. If anyone saw us together, and my parents came to know, I would be beaten black and blue and my classes would be stopped. After two hours, when I came out of the class, Raja was still there. He was sitting under a neem tree. I ignored him and started walking back. He did not try to stop me. For a full month, Raja followed me to my class, waited while I attended my lessons, and walked back behind me. He never said a word to me.

Then one day, when I came out of the class, Raja got up and walked off. Under the tree, I saw a red envelope. I looked around. No one was around in the three o'clock afternoon heat. So I walked to the tree, picked up the envelope and quickly put it inside my bag. I rushed home and opened it. There was a card. I did not know too much English, but I knew how to read the 'I love you' inside the heart on the card.

I wasn't sure what my response should be. Should I send him a note too? Or talk to him? In the end I did nothing. My dreams were full of Raja. I rehearsed in my mind what I would say to him when we did get around to talking.

Every day, Raja would leave me something under the tree. A note, a card, a piece of chocolate, a poem copied from somewhere, even a bottle of Thums Up. I was delighted, but never left anything for him. I knew how these Danda boys behaved. We called them 'Roadside Romeos'. They would pursue a girl and when she got friendly with them, they would ruin her reputation. I did not want that to happen to me.

One day, there was nothing from Raja for me, and he was nowhere to be seen. I was surprised at first. Then it occurred to me that he must have decided to chase another girl because I had not given him any attention. That made me sad. Little did he know that he dominated my thoughts.

When I got back to our lane, the place was teeming with a crowd and police. I saw Raja. He was all bloody. There was another guy, one of the 'Roadside Romeos' of Danda, laid out flat on his back. Raja's friends were also hurt, as were the other guy's friends. There were chains, broken bottles, and iron rods scattered on the road.

What had happened?

I sidled up to one of Raja's friends and asked him softly what had happened. He looked at me. In his eyes, there was deference and respect for me. He said gently, '*Didi*, the idiot Sunny said something cheap about you. Raja could not bear it and it became an all-out fight. Now Sunny has fainted, and the police have come to take Raja and Sunny to the police station.'

Raja fought for me? My heart bloomed like a million flowers when I heard that. He loves me so much that he feels honor bound to protect my reputation? I looked at Raja and saw him looking at me with a storm in his eyes. I smiled at him. I stood there till Sunny regained consciousness and both he and Raja were taken to the police station. Next day, Raja was back. When he followed me to my class, I waited till we got out of Danda. Then I stopped and when he caught up with me, we started walking together. We were together for three years, and then when Raja got his first job, his mother came home and met my parents. My parents were very angry that I had not told them about Raja. My reputation was already sullied because I had dared to fall in love, so they agreed to the marriage.

Anyway, what is done is done. Now, I had to beg for money all the time.

For some reason, I couldn't think of what to ask money for. I had just received my Diwali bonus, and lots of money from Piya madam's family. I had handed over the bonus money to Raja and told Piya madam to keep the ₹12,000 her family members had given me. I told her to save it for me for a rainy day. I decided to take that money back from Piya madam and tell Raja that she had given me only this much for a second-hand computer for our children. I also decided to tell him that she said that from now, I would have to pay back the advance in small installments and I would get the next advance only when the previous one was fully paid off.

I took the ₹12,000 from Piya madam and gave it to Raja. He beat me up real bad, and told me that I would have to look for another job. There was no reason to work at Piya madam's house anymore because she could not be relied upon for more money. I tried to tell him that I would have to work in four different houses to get the money that I got from Piya madam. He would not listen. So I told him to give me a week. I would ask Piya madam for more money.

I could not muster up the courage. I felt so ashamed. Yes, Raja was right. Piya madam had enough money to give me some. I managed her whole house. Yet, it did not seem right to ask for more. At the same time I did not want to leave her. She was better than most employers. She did not nitpick or nag me about small things.

I worried about what to do. How to ask for more money.

One day, as I was dusting Piya madam's room, I saw a beautiful ring in her bedside drawer. It had a large yellow stone in the middle and white stones surrounding it. I had worked long enough in rich houses to know that the ring was an expensive one. Piya madam had got it a few months ago, and had shown it to me. She was delighted with it, but told me to not talk about it in front of Anand sir. She said, 'I have bought it for myself and have not told Anand yet. So keep quiet about it.'

I smiled and said yes. Piya madam told me many things, and I told her things in my life too. She knew I would not betray her trust.

Now when I saw the ring, an awful thought entered my head. I tried to brush it away but it kept nagging me. I could take the ring. And Piya madam would not be able to raise a stink about it. At night when I was in bed, I thought about the ring again. If I took the ring, Piya madam would know it was me. She had shown me the ring. The whole night I tossed and turned dreaming about the ring.

Two days later when I got to work, there was mayhem in the household. Piya madam was still in her night clothes, and she was furious. Anand sir was also still at home. The whole house was in disarray—books were strewn everywhere, the clothes were out of the cupboard, and the sheets and bedding were off the bed. Piya madam looked at me and said, 'Gudia, my jewelry and money are missing.'

I looked at her in horror and put my hand to my mouth. 'Oh no, what happened? What has gone missing?'

—My gold bangles and ₹10,000 from my purse.

'Piya madam. I have not taken those things. I have worked for 10 years in your house,' I blurted out.

Piya madam looked up and said crossly, 'Of course it is not you. I know you. But who can it be? All of it has been stolen between yesterday afternoon and this morning.'

—Who could it be?

—You tell me Gudia. This Sheela won't stop crying. Who all came home yesterday?

I was sweating. My forehead was moist and I could feel the wetness in my armpits too. I fumbled, 'The driver came in the evening with the mutton. The cleaning *bai* came in the afternoon to clean the bathrooms. The girls' music teacher came for their lesson too. And then Ayesha madam's kids came to play and they were with their maid.'

—Who entered my room?

—I went in to dust. And the cleaning *bai* for sweeping and mopping. Sheela went to your room to put away the ironed clothes. That's all.

Piya madam said softly, 'You think any of the other two stole my things?'

I gulped, 'I don't think so madam. I was around all the time.'

Anand sir said something in rapid English to Madam. I am not sure what he said, because I can't keep up with such fast English. Maybe he said that she should not absolve me of suspicion. Or maybe he said she should not pressure me.

Piya madam called in Sheela, 'Why are you crying Sheela? Did you steal my bangles?'

At this, Sheela started crying even louder and between sobs she said, 'No madam. I swear on my mother I did not.'

—Please stop swearing on your mother all the time. You have stolen in the past.

—Yes I did, but not this time. You can check my bags.

Piya madam turned to me. 'Gudia, please go and check her bags.'

My heart was thumping wildly and I brought out Sheela's bag. I said, 'Let me check it in front of you madam.'

I took out the things from Sheela's bag. In the last few months, her assets had increased. Piya madam had given her new clothes and new *chappals*. From the salary Sheela earned every month, she got to keep ₹200 while the rest was sent back home to her parents. From her money she had bought small things for herself—a bottle of shampoo, talcum powder, a *kajal* pencil, a shiny lip gloss, *bindis,* and some trinkets. I opened the box of trinkets. It had some glass and metal bangles, some earrings, and a gaudy gold-plated necklace. Her much-used undergarments came out of the bag next. As did a small piece of washing soap. A purse that Piya madam had given her. There was nothing else in the bag.

Piya madam said, 'Open the purse.'

My hands trembled as I opened the purse. Out came four thick gold bangles that were Piya madam's, and some money. Mutely, I handed those to madam. Sheela was hysterical. 'I swear Madam. I have not seen these things ever. I did not steal them. I promise. May my mother die if I am lying.'

I saw the fury in madam's eyes being replaced with sadness. She looked at Sheela with pity and said, 'Pack your things Sheela. I will settle your account. You must leave in 15 minutes.'

She told me, 'Check the bag once more and see if we missed anything. There is only ₹5,000 here and two gold bangles are still missing. They should be here too.'

I checked the bag once more, and shook my head. There was nothing more here. 'She must have given the bangles and money to someone else.'

Anand sir got up and went to his room. Piya madam looked at him leave, and then whispered to me, 'The ring is missing too.'

I looked at her with surprise on my face.

—It is not here madam.

Piya madam's face fell. She looked so sad, as if she had lost a part of herself. She said softly, 'Let it be. It was not meant to be. Don't mention it in front of Anand.'

I nodded.

I watched as Sheela put her meager belongings in her bag. I felt bad for her.

—*Didi*, I don't know how those things came in my bag. Madam does

not believe me, but I swear on my mother. Where will I go now?
—Don't worry Sheela, you will get a job. There is a madam on Mount Mary who was looking for someone. You call me tomorrow. I will check with her this afternoon.
—*Didi*, I was really happy here.
I commiserated with her. My heart felt very heavy.
I went through the day with great sadness in my heart. And when I returned home in the evening and sat with the other ladies in the *chawl*, I felt great stress.
I had never stolen in my life. Up until now. People suspect the household help when anything goes missing, but Piya madam did not even think for a minute that I could have been the thief. I had broken her trust. Fear and embarrassment make us behave in bad ways. I was stuck between the fire and the frying pan. If I did not get the money I would have lost this house to work in. And been brutally beaten.
When I had walked into the house two days ago, I had a plan in my mind. I decided to steal the gold bangles and the ring. As well as the money. Rich people think that gold is the only valuable thing that poor people are aware of. And of money. The truth is, we know a lot more. We watch as the ladies of the house flaunt their diamonds and other shiny stones. We overhear conversations. Sheela was the unfortunate collateral damage. Piya madam would believe that Sheela had stolen the gold and money. She was new to the work, and very poor. She hardly got any money to keep with herself because her parents took away all of it. She had stolen the girls' trinkets in the past, so it was only natural that she would try her hand on madam's jewelry as she understood the household better.
So I stole the bangles and the money. I put four bangles and half the money in Sheela's purse when she went down to the play area with the girls. I tied the other two gold bangles, the ring, and ₹5,000 in a small napkin and quickly sewed it on to one of my panties. I wore this panty on top of the one I was already wearing when I walked off for the day.
I sold one bangle and gave Raja ₹10,000. Oh how his mean face

shone. He smirked at me, 'See I told you that if you threatened to leave, she would give you all that you wanted.'

I smiled at him. What could I say?

I still had one bangle and the ring with me. They were hidden at the bottom of the container that had rice in it. I know no one touched that ever.

I bought myself some peace of mind with what I stole. The next time Raja would demand more money, I would simply sell the bangle and give him the money. The ring was risky business. I wish I had not taken it. In the jewelry shops we frequented, the shopkeepers did not deal in these kinds of stones. And I didn't know the price of the ring, so there was a chance I could get cheated and receive very little money. Maybe one day, I will wear a new sari and go to Juhu or Santacruz and check at the jewelry stores there. I could speak a fair amount of English, so I could pretend to be a middle-class housewife. If they gave me a good rate I should be able to sell it. And keep the money hidden away.

Of course, I will still asked Piya madam periodically for money. Else she might suspect me. She may think that if I am not asking for money, it is because I stole from her.

She knew the callous way Raja treated me. Like I knew that ring was a gift from the *sahib* she was constantly on the phone with some months ago. I had never seen her happier. And then, after she got back alive from that Taj Hotel nightmare (thank God), she was the saddest I had ever seen. I knew the *sahib* stopped calling her, because I never heard that chirpiness in her voice again. The only phone calls she got were for work, and from her other friends. She cried a lot in those days.

Some things you don't have to be told. A woman's heart can understand.

Veera

The beauty of being young. You forget.

There was so much happening in my life at that time, that today I can't seem to remember if I missed Ravi too much. I must have. Bandstand suddenly felt so lonely. I would walk down with KD every single evening, and sit on the same old bench and think of Ravi.

He never quite left my thoughts, and he left me with many wonderful gifts. I started making an effort to talk to people, to make friends. And before long, I had many—my Bandstand friends as I called them. Mostly young girls like me, who stayed at home and took care of kids. And when we started sharing our experiences, I realized I was not alone in my misery at home. Most of us were in loveless marriages—married to nice, decent human beings, but with no love.

There was duty and loyalty, but the things that held us together were societal pressure, financial dependence, and most importantly, the children. We all dreamed big for our children, we wanted them to be successful; we wanted them to do far better than us. Today's generation likes to think they have invented love, commitment, ambition. That they 'struggle' through bad marriages. That they have ambitions for their kids. Little do they know.

My Bandstand friends were the first family I had. And most of them remained part of my life for many years.

And so time passed, the ordinary routine that each day churned out, till one day, a phone call changed my life. No one ever called for me, so when Gurujitji called me and told me I had a call, I was taken aback. If it had been Veerji, Gurujitji would have spoken to him first. I took the call with great trepidation. At the other end was a woman. She said someone had told her that I was a very good cook. Their daughter had recently moved to Bandra from Delhi, and would I please cook for her and deliver a *dabba* every evening? I didn't know what to say, so I told the lady I would call her back next day. When I hung up, Gurujitji was watching me and asked me who it was. I told him about the conversation. *Maaji* was hovering around and said, 'Who said these lies about you? Anyway, doesn't matter, you cannot cook for other people. You barely manage to do your own work.'

Thank god Gurujitji was there. He said, 'Let her do it *maaji*. It is time she did something for herself.'

—Have your brains gone to the dogs? Which girl in our family has gone out to work? It sends out the wrong signal—that you don't earn enough money to support your own family.

Gurujitji sighed, 'Those days are gone *maaji*. And she is not stepping out of the house to work. She will do it right here. I will find someone who can drop and pick up the *dabba* from the girl's house. Many women do this from home, and it is a good way to earn some money too.'

Maaji fumed, 'So we have suddenly become modern? We must now live off the earnings of our womenfolk? Should I also go out of the house and work?'

Gurujitji sighed. 'Times are changing *maaji*.'

—Next thing you will say 'let her join the movies and become an actress'! You have gone mad, Guru. This girl has always turned your mind. You kept a barren woman for years and refused to marry again. Now you want to let her work and earn her own money. Were you ever in control of your marriage?

Gurujitji said, 'Would you have liked it if one of my sisters could not conceive and her husband sent her back? Is that our upbringing? And anyway, this argument is pointless. I have anyway made up my mind; she *will* do this *dabba*.'

Again, like he had done in the past, Gurujitji stood up for me and *maaji* could say no more.

Sometimes, when I think of Gurujitji now, I think he must have cared for me in his own way. Loved me too. We did not belong to a generation that said 'I love you' as casually as today's children do. When KD leaves home in the morning, he always kisses Mana and says 'I love you'. When Piya hangs up the phone after talking to Anand, it is always with a 'love you babes'. Kids tell their parents that they love them, parents tell them they love them. My grandkids tell me they love me and I say it to them too.

I did not see it then, but I now realize that love takes many different forms. I did not understand Gurujitji's way of loving. I thought it was his duty and honor, but perhaps it was love that made him not marry a second time, that made him let me work when it was not the 'done' thing in most families.

I had wanted a different love. One where I could snuggle into someone's arms and rest my head on his shoulder. One where the person would protect me against *maaji* and stand up for me. A love that would appreciate me for what I was. I wanted a love where I could go on long walks, splash in the rain on Bandstand, share *bhel puri* from the same plate, talk about my childhood, talk about my dreams for my kids, laugh, giggle at our private jokes, and be held with affection. That's why I love it when my kids are so demonstrative with their spouses. It is such a blessing, to be loved like that.

I loved Gurujitji, don't misunderstand that. It was a love that was borne out of gratitude—that he was a decent human being, did not trouble me, and did not leave me for another woman in all those years when I could not give him a child, did not hit me, and did not criticize my parents. Maybe for our times, that kind of love was enough. Just not enough for me.

My mind runs off with thoughts. I was telling you about how I started working. The very next day I called the woman and told her I would make a *dabba* for her daughter and have it delivered. Gurujitji left me some money and I went to the store on Hill Road to buy a brand new *dabba*.

Oh the pleasure I felt in picking out that shiny blue *dabba*! I had never bought anything for the house because *maaji* was in charge, so this made me giddy with happiness, almost as if I was setting up home myself. Now I have lost count of the number of *dabbas* and the innumerable meals I have catered in the years gone by, but I still remember that first meal I packed. That *dabba* had *bhindi*, *aloo* curry, a portion of rice, three *chapattis*, three cucumber slices and two tomato roundels as salad, a piece of peanut *chikki*, and some *saunf*. I said a little prayer to Guru Nanak before I started cooking and my first earnings went into the money box at the Dhan Potohar Gurudwara.

And just like that, in such a small way, my 'business' took off. Before the month was over, I was packing 10 *dabbas* every day, and before the year was over, it was up to 50 every single night. I was busy, and oh so happy. I was earning money, and dutifully handed over all of it to Gurujitji. He would remove money for expenses, and put the balance in a bank account for me. He was the one who insisted that I get help to cut and chop vegetables and other ingredients, so I employed an additional maid. *Maaji* was furious! The tiny house was overrun with vegetables, *masalas*, *dabbas*, and an additional person in the small kitchen. Oh the tantrums she would throw! I couldn't care less. I was so happy. The Chimbai house finally felt like my own home. My mind was always buzzing with what I was going to cook the next day. And how I could make the *dabba* different and yet delicious every single day. I delivered Namita in all this chaos and Piya followed two years later. I was never busier, or happier, than I was in those years.

I tried to replicate what I remembered of my Rawalpindi kitchen. I would buy whole spices, roast them, and then grind them for cooking. Even now, I love the aroma of *dhania, jeera, kali mirchi, methi dana,* and *lal mirchi* being roasted and ground into a fine powder. (Now our Khar kitchen, where all the cooking for catering takes place, is redolent with the smells of other spices—*panch poren,* allspice, star anise, *galangal,* basil, truffles; as many spices as the cuisines we serve up now.)

I used only the best ingredients and the freshest meats and vegetables. Soon, the vendors in the *mandi* knew me well enough to know what I wanted, and the poultry and butcher shop would reserve the best cuts for me. I was overwhelmed with the generosity of the people around me. The grocers would give me credit for the month, my Bandstand friends would share their family recipes with me, and the delivery boys would come back with information on what other *dabbawallahs* were serving so I knew what the competition was doing.

And my children were accommodating. They grew up with the smells of cooking in the house and loved it. Even as a young girl, Namita would sit on the floor and shell the peas. KD was an expert at slicing, chopping, and grating onions. Piya would gather all the vegetables and set up her own shop in the corridor as the vegetable vendor. Children are so simple. They create a game out of anything they find.

I must confess they were quite deprived of a wholesome breakfast before school. In the morning I would be in a rush to go to the *mandi* to pick up fresh vegetables and meats for the evening meal. I would pack their tiffins with leftovers from the previous night and hand them a glass of milk and a banana, or a fruit bun or some bread-butter-jam as breakfast. Not once did the three complain. When they returned in the afternoon from school, I used to have something nice ready for them. *Poha, dosas, vada pav*, noodles. I had time then—after the chopping and grating was done, and just before the cooking would begin for the *dabbas* to be delivered for the evening meal.

One evening, almost a year after I had started the *dabba* service, Gurujitji said that his *sethji* wanted me to cater the *puja* service they were having in the office. I had to cook the food and have it delivered to the office. *Maaji* was livid. She said Gurujitji was living off my earnings and what pathetic man would behave like that. Gurujitji, in his soft voice, told *maaji* that she could leave the house and live with his sisters if she was unhappy. Thinking of her face that day can still bring a smile to my face. She looked like a fish gasping for water. Her mouth opened, shut, opened, shut, and then remained shut forever. Trust me, I did not feel happy about it. To see her power decimated in this manner. But I didn't mind it either. I had suffered enough and did not want her to ever trouble me again.

Did I mention that even in the years she had troubled me so much, I got my revenge in small little ways? After every beating, I would spit into the dough with which I rolled out *chapattis* for *maaji*. She was a strict vegetarian so I would mix some chicken curry in her vegetable curry and watch her eat it with relish. I never felt guilty—not one bit. And I never got caught. She chose to hurt me; I just got back at her. Looking back it all seems so seamless. Doing *dabbas*, getting into catering—beginning with just cooking and delivering, and then expanding to do almost everything else. It wasn't like that though. That time was fraught with a lot of insecurity. I never wanted to do anything wrong or imperfect, so I put in a lot of energy in it. *Maaji* refused to help me even with the kids, so I had to bear that burden too. I wanted to do so much more, but I had only two hands. We hired more people to help me with the cutting and chopping, but I mixed the *masalas* myself and kept the information to the exact recipe to myself.

Piya, my youngest one, always helped me out. By the time she was 14, she was accompanying me on purchases, negotiating deals, and planning meals and menus. She joined the Institute of Hotel Management in Mumbai to understand the business better. I also insisted that she join some professional cooking courses. Times were changing. I had made a successful business with traditional home-style Punjabi cooking, but in order to survive and grow, we needed to understand other cuisines too. By then, KD was working, and we had moved out of our Chimbai house. We used that house as the kitchen. There was money to spare. So off Piya went to Paris where she spent three months learning the fine art of French cooking and presentation. We sent her to the Culinary School of America in New York to hone her baking skills. She also went to Bangkok and stayed with KD's friend and learnt Thai cooking. That's where she met Anand—and they got married just as she got more involved in the business.

When Mana came into the family, I finally began to relax. She had a flair for this business too, and together she and Piya have managed it so well. It is all very different from what I started, but my girls are wonderful at it. Thanks to them I could put up my feet and enjoy my life. KD insists on taking me on family holidays, but I always tell him that three generations traveling together is not such a great idea. The kids want to do something more adventurous, and I like to while my time away—walking aimlessly, sitting in a roadside café, watching people go by, or go to an *ayurveda* ashram where I get pampered with massages and treatments. I like my alone time, and I think I have earned it!

I know it is bad karma to even think like this, but really, when Gurujitji passed on, I felt liberated. Liberated that I did not have to spend my life the rest of my life with a man I did not love. I was not young anymore—I was 50. I had spent almost 37 years being married to someone I did not want to be with. I liked him, respected him, and was grateful to him—in many ways, he saved my life. He cared about me and yet, like all good things in my life, he expressed it too late. By then I had paid my debts to him too, and by going early, he released me from any further burden.

I enjoyed my widowhood. I was still young and had my own money. I got KD and Piya married, was there with them when my grandkids were born, saw my three children become successful, made friends who gave me an active social life. I lived life queen size.

I never forgot Ravi though. We had unfinished business.

Namita

To: Piyar@gmail.com
From: namitap@gmail.com
Jul 2, 2013
8.15 p.m.

The shoot is wrapping up and I will reach Mumbai on Friday evening. Will come directly to the hospital.
Rahul is also coming to Mumbai this weekend. Cross your fingers and pray for me.

To: namitap@gmail.com
From: Piyar@gmail.com
July 2, 2013
11 p.m.

Oh thank god you are coming Nams. I am pretty sure Mom will get up when you come back. I get the feeling she is waiting for you.

Don't worry. I have a good feeling about you and Rahul! Btw, he connected with me on FB yesterday. A simple statement that he was looking forward to meeting us all.

To: Piyar@gmail.com
From: namitap@gmail.com
Jul 2, 2013
11.03 p.m.

I hope so Piya.
After Kal, I have found it very hard to trust someone. I don't hold a grudge against Kal, but should Garima have done this to me? She was my best friend. What kind of girl eyes her best friend's boyfriend? And marries him, despite knowing that he dumped me when I was pregnant?

To: namitap@gmail.com
From: Piyar@gmail.com
Jul 2, 2013
11.20 p.m.

Ya man Namita, that was terrible. I see Kal and Garima at Otter's Club once in a while. Whenever she sees me, she has a silly grin on her face, and pointedly puts her hand on Kal. I find it so juvenile. What does she think? That I care? In the initial days post your break-up, Kal tried to contact Anand, KD, Mana and me. None of us ever responded. Did he really think that he would keep his place in our lives after what he had done to you? Or that we would even care enough to listen to his sob story? What audacity!
You should give Rahul a deeper thought though. If both of you decide to be together, it will be so wonderful! You told me once that you wanted to marry a friend. Well, with Rahul you have enough history. And he was one of your best friends. What more can you want? You won't be choosing to be with him because you have not found anyone else. Hell Namita, I know so many men who want you. You are beautiful, intelligent, successful. Some just want access to KD through you. At least you

know Rahul wants you only for yourself.

To: Piyar@gmail.com
From: namitap@gmail.com
Jul 3, 2013
1 a.m.

Maybe you are right Piya. And even if nothing comes of it, at least I will have my best friend back in my life.
Maybe it is time for fresh beginnings. With Mom as well...maybe I can have a less fractured relationship with her.

Veera

Abandonment is hard to define. When I look back now, the times I thought I was abandoned were not such bad times. Being in Gurujitji's house, being troubled by *maaji* and my family not coming to my rescue—it was bad, but bearable. Not being able to have children for 14 long years, being spited for that and kept out of all joyous occasions—that too was not so bad. Ravi never seeking me out, after all we had shared—not so bad.

I felt true abandonment when Veerji passed away. He was the constant presence in my life from my childhood. *Beyji* never came to visit me in my marital home. You know how it was in the olden days—you would not even have a glass of water in your daughter's home. After KD was born, I did visit my parents in Delhi but was there for precious little time. I had a budding business, three kids, and a home to take care of. Veerji visited me every year. In his eyes I saw the distress and anger at the way I was treated being replaced by pride at the business I was building. He was so proud of me, and in his wallet he always carried a picture of me.

I saw my Veerji grow old. He looked even more handsome as the years went by, with his salt-and-pepper beard and the gentleness on his face. He stood by me when I married off my children. In Veerji, I had a home. And when he died, a part of me died with him. Now there was no one who cared about my tears, my smile, my concerns. No one who I could share my childhood memories with. No one who hugged me so tight that his big muscular body trembled with emotion.

That is abandonment. When you feel bereft of the people who loved you for what you were. Who have seen you from your childhood and know all the things you loved and cared about. Who else would have remembered that I was a young girl once? That I scraped my knees too, and *beyji* would give me some *gur shakar* to calm me down? That I had climbed a guava tree and hidden there once because I had beaten up some boys in school and was scared that I would be punished at home? Who would know that I used to hide my candy under the mattress and was stingy with it? That I secretly picked my nose when I thought no one was looking? Who remembered that I loved two heaped teaspoons of sugar in my milk and would feed the strays my *chapattis*? Who remembered *baaji's* stories with me? Or that house in Rawalpindi?

When Veerji died, my stories died with him. That is loneliness. I became only Veera—mother to KD, Namita and Piya. No one even knows why I was called Veera. Or that my full name was Veerawali—the blessed one with a brother. They were all gone.

My hollowness increased the day I met Ravi again, after decades. It was almost 10 years ago, if I remember correctly. I had gone with my family for dinner, and while we waited for our car to come, I noticed a handsome, distinguished man come into the lobby. With a start I realized it was Ravi. I went up to him and said hesitantly, 'Ravi?'

Ravi was startled at first and then his face creased into the smile I had remembered for so many years. He said, 'Veera! It's you after so many years!' And he moved to give me a hug. In his delight, he turned to his family and said, 'Sangeeta, you remember Veera? After so many years! What a surprise!'

He had married Sangeeta? I noticed the rest of his family then. Sangeeta, elegant and pretty. His two sons, who had the good-looking genes of both the parents. Sangeeta nodded at me and said, 'Of course I remember her. How are you Veera?' She smiled but her eyes held no warmth.

Ravi held my hands in his. 'How have you been Veera? You disappeared one fine day. I sent Sangeeta to speak to you, but you refused to meet her. Did I do something wrong? What were you upset about?'

I didn't meet Sangeeta?

I smiled, 'It was so long ago Ravi. I don't even remember. I was not too well. When I came back to Bandstand, you were no longer there.'

Ravi said, 'I had to rush back to Delhi because my father had fallen sick. That's why I had asked Sangeeta to meet you. I came back to Mumbai three years later, and went to Bandstand to look for you, but did not find you.'

If you really wanted to, you would have found me. And what can I say about not meeting Sangeeta? What did you want her to tell me? After so many years, what good will the truth do to us? That I sent a letter telling you everything? That I waited for you?

I did not reply to that. Instead, I introduced him to my children. I watched him shake hands with my children and make small talk with them. I thought, *he will never know the truth.*

'You look lovely Veera,' he then said to me.

KD, my proud KD, put his arms around my shoulders and boasted, 'She is a hotshot businesswoman and runs one of the most successful catering firms in Mumbai.'

Ravi's face lit up. 'I can well imagine that. Your mother fed me the best *paranthas* and *chhole* when I was in Mumbai. I never forgot the flavor.'

'Ravi I am sure you are responsible for this. I think you had asked someone to call me for a *dabba*. Someone from Delhi. That's how I started.'

Ravi gave me an inscrutable smile. 'Maybe. You were so good at it.

I'm so happy about your success Veera. You deserve every bit of it.'
KD gave him my visiting card. I saw Ravi hold it lovingly and run his fingers along the edges.

—You call it 'Jugalbandi'!

—In your honor, Ravi. Remember?

He said quietly, 'I remember. Everything.'

Jugalbandi.

The first time he used that word was the first time Ravi made love to me. We were in his apartment, and KD had gone off to sleep. He had gotten drenched in the rain at Bandstand, and I changed him and gave him milk in Ravi's apartment. Ravi handed me my tea and then, just as simple as that, kissed me on my lips. After we were done he said, 'Jugalbandi. That should be the name of your restaurant. A mix of beautiful flavors. A coming together of unlikely things—like you and me, and creating a beautiful world all of our own.'

Like I said, love can take different forms. And each satisfies a deep part of one's soul. Ravi was in my life for the briefest of times, but his gifts to me were so many. He gave me love. He gave me my first *dabba* assignment. He believed in me.

He gave me Namita.

Sangeeta stood listening to everything. I only smiled.

What could I tell him? That he did not even recognize what fruit our own '*jugalbandi*' had borne? That my Namita was truly a unique mix of his flavors and mine. Had he looked closely, he would have been struck by how Namita resembled him—she had his curly hair, his smile, his body structure. Her heart was where her father's had been—in art and photography.

That was the reason I was so against Namita taking up photography. I had loved Ravi, but years of silence had whittled away my love. No love lasts forever, except for the love of one's children. My bitterness against him made me want to keep his daughter away from everything he held dear. I did not even want her to be part of the company I had named when I still felt love for him. We stood around chatting a while longer. Ravi was in Mumbai to meet his boys who stayed here now. All of us made polite noises about meeting up again. There was a sour taste in my mouth.

In my heart, I knew I would never meet Ravi again. He could never know about Namita. I wondered about Sangeeta though. How she must have been in love with Ravi to lie to him. To tell him I had never met her. To not give him the letter I had entrusted her to give him. I did not feel betrayed by Sangeeta. She was never my friend, and I knew even then that she was in love with Ravi. She did what she had to, to make Ravi hers. Our lives could have been so different if Ravi had got that letter. Maybe he would have taken me to Delhi, or maybe he would have left me. At least he would have known the truth about Namita.

Did Sangeeta know the truth? Had she read the letter? Did she wonder when she met my children which one could be Ravi's? Did she feel anything at all?

I realized I did not care anymore.

As time goes by, so many things become unimportant. At one time I had wanted to tell Ravi the truth about Namita. I hated myself for living a life of lies. I felt horrible when Gurujitji held the little baby in his arms for the first time and whispered, 'She is Namita, our unpretentious and humble one.' I felt like the biggest cheat when people said she looked like Gurujitji. I prayed and prayed to Guru Nanak. I had sinned, but I did not want the truth to come out. I did not want Namita to pay for my mistakes. I think Guru Nanak protected me. My secret is safe. Now, I don't see a reason to explain. No good can come of it.

Like no good would have come from my telling Gurujitji the truth about her. I gave my three children a stable, happy childhood with Gurujitji, who loved them all deeply. Namita has two siblings who love her intensely. She is part of this family.

Like no good will come from telling Namita about her real father. She loved Gurujitji and was more attached to him than KD or Piya were. She was his true daughter.

Human beings are strange creatures. They can live a whole life—a happy and fulfilling one—while dreaming of another that could have been. Another that they wanted, with their heart and soul.

The day I met Ravi, my abandonment was complete. The what-ifs and what-might-have-beens disappeared.

The day I met him, I felt old.

Simran

There are times in your life that you think you will not survive what you are going through; that this is the worst phase of your life. My experience—no one dies of a broken heart, or for that matter, of a heart that stops feeling after some time. Through it all, you survive. And after some time, you begin to live. And then, you begin to see the beauty in someone's smile, the honesty in someone's compliments, the truth in someone's concern for you. You begin to see the beauty in your own self—when you look at the mirror, you begin to like the face that stares back at you. You begin to appreciate yourself.

You begin to look at yourself beyond the slurs of slut, prostitute, and loose woman.

You begin to be you.

This is my last day in Mumbai and I am almost done tying up all the loose ends. The packers were done last week itself and I have been staying at the Grand Hyatt for the last few days.

At the farewell party in the office last night, when I was called upon to give a speech, I said all the right things—how great it had been to spend this last year with an intelligent, creative set of people, how I would cherish those memories, and how I looked forward to working with some of them back in New York in the near future. What I did not talk about was the fact that I was leaving behind someone I loved very much, someone whose life I would never be a part of. I would miss the person. But this was a choice I had made. And I hope the sacrifice is worth it.

I am waiting to say goodbye. At a table in the coffee shop from where I can see people in the lobby, I order a cup of herbal tea. I look at all the busy bees—the office head honchos at lunch or interview meetings, the kitty-party ladies with their Fendis and Salvatore Ferragamos— and I think of 'Sonder'. KD had mentioned it to me once, and I am having that moment now. The realization that each of these people has a life as vivid and complex as mine. Each of them has their set of relationships, routines, and weirdness. Each person has a story that I will never be privy to, and connections to thousands of other lives that I will never know. Maybe this is my moment in their lives, sitting at a table, sipping my tea, a wallflower, an extra on a movie set! Completely unmemorable, forgettable.

I leave Mumbai with sadness this time. Nothing to bind me to this city anymore. My parents died a few years ago. I did not keep in touch with my school or college friends. Only one person mattered. But there is no going back on what has been, and no way to stay connected—in public at least.

Fifteen years ago, I was the happiest person when I was packing up to leave Mumbai to join my new husband in London.

I met Jaiveer at my cousin's wedding. Fresh out of my MFA from UCLA, I was contemplating joining an advertising firm in India, because mother wanted me back to get married to a good Indian boy. She was not too delighted that Taps came to India with me.

A gorgeous Cuban, with thick bushy eyebrows, a taut body, and an amazing sense of humor, Taps and I had been together for more than a year. We were great friends, and had sort of stumbled into a committed relationship. I was deeply fond of him, though I had not yet thought of marriage and how my parents would respond to a Cuban son-in-law. Taps wanted to see India and he was delighted with everything in Mumbai. My friends loved him and we were out partying every night. Life was fun. Taps and friends, parties, booze... everything a young girl might want.

Then I met Jaiveer and I was smitten. Oh My God. He was incredibly handsome. I had never looked at turbaned Sikh boys as potential boyfriends, but Jaiveer blew my mind. He was a smart dresser, wonderfully articulate, and had an amazing aura about him. In a place like Mumbai, where the hotel staff fusses over you only if you are a Bollywood star, he was treated like royalty. I noticed him as soon as he had walked into the cocktail party, but when he made a beeline for me, and stuck to me all evening, I couldn't believe my luck. Sure, I knew I was looking nice in my royal blue *lehnga* with its intricate gold embroidery. But there were girls lovelier than me and he didn't pay them any attention. All evening I wondered how it would be to kiss him. I had never kissed anyone with a beard before. Would it be prickly? Would there be hair all over my mouth? My tongue? It sounded gross, but I wanted it nonetheless.

Jaiveer had moved from India right after college and worked hard to set up a successful retail business in London. He owned and operated a chain of pharmacies and sandwich shops. He was expanding his business into commercial properties and hotels in London.

Jaiveer laid it on thick. He was in Mumbai for a week, and every single day he took me out. Sometimes we went out with friends, but mostly we were alone. Jaiveer wanted to know everything about me. It can be so charming—to be with someone who is besotted with you, and wants to be with you all the time. I didn't even think of Taps who was furious with me. I left him sulking with friends.

I had only Jaiveer on my mind.

We women are such suckers for successful men and what they seem to represent. To me Jaiveer became the future I had always wanted. I wanted a house in a tony London suburb, a fancy car to drive, loads of nice branded clothes, shoes and jewelry. My parents would approve of this handsome, rich *Serdi* boy.

A five-carat ring and a residence in Kensington Park—that was the price of my freedom.

I see Mana walk in. In her pink *kurti* and white trousers she looks lovely. She is on the phone, and from a distance, it seems to me that someone is literally on the receiving end. Her eyes seek me out. She raises her hand and signals me to wait for five.

When I moved to London I was so delighted. A five-bedroom colonial house just off Kensington. A swanky Mercedes sedan. A handsome husband. A husband who was besotted with me. I got a job with an advertising agency as a creative intern and life began on a dream note.

Jaiveer was a good lover. I know because I have had men in my life. UCLA abounded with gorgeous men. And I had my share of admirers. I had a great time. I wasn't in love with any of the men I had been with, and it never got messy.

When Jaiveer made love to me the first time, my body reacted to him with passion. He looked at me through a lust-laden haze and said, 'Have you slept with other men?' A warning bell rang in my head, and I murmured coyly, 'No. I haven't, my love'. For the rest of the night, I waited impatiently as he 'taught' me how to do things that pleased him. How to hold him, how to go down on him. I learnt to withhold my moves when he touched me, and made love to me.

I had to behave like a 'good' Indian girl who had been a virgin till she got married.

Like I said—he was good.

I didn't think life could get any better for me. I had it all. Or at least, I thought I had it all.

One evening, in the first month of our marriage, we were invited to a party. I wore a full-length pale green gown, which looked good on me. Jaiveer held my arm firmly when we entered. Soon, I was caught up meeting his friends. They were delighted to meet me and had so many stories about him to share. I had a few drinks, and there was Bollywood music to dance to. It was such a heady feeling—to be married to the best guy in the room, and to be the envy of all the other women there. By the time we came back home I was happily tipsy and slept even before I could change my clothes.

The next morning, I woke up deliriously happy. I changed my clothes and walked out of our room. Jaiveer was sitting calmly at the table, eating his breakfast of eggs, bacon and bread. I went up to him to kiss him. He was unresponsive.

I asked him what was wrong. He said nothing as he made his way through his eggs and bread. I sat next to him and playfully poked him with my finger. 'What's up my darling husband?'

I was stunned when the orange juice hit my face. I looked at Jaiveer in surprise and said, 'What the hell? What's wrong?'

That beautiful face disintegrated into something ugly as he said, 'I should have never married you. You are a slut.'

I was baffled. *What had I done?*

—You are a bloody whore. You left Taps for me. And now you want fresh blood.

What the hell was he talking about? Anger took over. I was so furious, I lunged at him. And Jaiveer smacked me, right across my face. I looked at him shellshocked. *What is wrong with him? What does he think he is doing?*

He crushed my face between his palms. Funny how I had never noticed that his palms were thick and fleshy. *Like a laborer*, I thought. His eyes bore into me and he hissed, 'I married a whore.'

I could feel the beginnings of a headache. And fear. 'What did I do? I partied with your friends? Where did I do anything?'

He said, 'I saw the way your body was reacting to every guy there. Wanting to be touched.'

—You're crazy!

—You bloody slut!

And the next thing I knew, he had grabbed my hair and hit me on my face. I tried to scramble out of his grip but he was so much stronger. I started screaming in fury and pain. And he hit me more. With unbelievable strength, and uncontrolled anger. When he was done, I hurt all over.

I don't know what hurt more. My body that felt like pulp. Or my heart, that couldn't understand what was wrong.

I crawled back into bed and wept all morning.

You hear of domestic violence and how victims believe they are the perpetrators. They deserve to be beaten. It took me no time at all to believe the same. I tried to find answers to why a loving guy like Jaiveer would change into this monster. Maybe he got agitated with the way I behaved at the party. I *was* a natural flirt. I was used to attention and I enjoyed it. Maybe I had behaved badly.

When Jaiveer came back that evening, I dressed up in a simple dress and waited for him. I cooked us a nice meal. I hugged him and apologized. Told him I would never behave badly again. Jaiveer merely looked at me and said, 'Good.'

That night, his lovemaking was different. Punishing. Bruising. He made love to me as if he hated me. Couldn't bear to touch me. His lovemaking made me feel like a slut.

I had read that when a guy hits you, he feels remorse later. Jaiveer felt none. And I got hit again and again. Over simple things—like the tea not being hot enough. Or the bed not being made properly. Or the car not being parked properly. He stopped me from going to work. No amount of cajoling would make him agree to my going to work. He thought I was looking to prostitute myself.

Jaiveer still wanted me to keep up his social obligations and made it clear that it would be disastrous if I misbehaved. I learnt to change the way I dressed. I began to wear looser clothing that would not show off my curves. I learnt to not chat animatedly with anyone because it would bring on a volley of blows to my ribs. Very soon, people stopped including me in their conversations. I mean, who would have found me attractive? I had nothing to contribute, nothing to say because an untoward comment would mean a beating. I took up no offers of meeting the other ladies for coffee because Jaiveer would not like it.

You cannot imagine the loneliness one can feel in a room full of people. You sit there, observing everyone, trying to assess who it is you can confide in. Men. Women. And it hits you that they are not your friends. That's just what happened to me, like textbook 101 on domestic abuse. All 'our' friends were first and only Jaiveer's friends. They would only take his side and believe what he said. They had known him for a long time and would never believe he was a wife beater. He was rich and powerful, and everyone curried favor with him.

I was lonely. Alone in my grief. There was no one I could talk to. My friends in India were upset because they blamed me for dumping Taps. I could not tell my parents and worry them. I could not reach out to Taps. He would have understood, but I had burned my bridges with him and hurt him deeply.

I began to eat copious amounts of food. All day at home that's what I did—eat, and watch mindless TV. Jaiveer viewed my body with even more disgust. And to mask the hurt I ate more. I became fat and ugly. I would look at myself in the mirror and hate my body. Gone was that taut body that looked good in all clothes. Gone was that pretty face that charmed people. Gone was the light in my eyes. Gone was my smile.

You reach a point in your life when you think life can't get any worse. That you will be able to live with the disaster your life has turned out to be. You lower your expectations and your dreams. I thought I could live this life indefinitely too.

Until Jaiveer started bringing women home. Sexy, smart young things that he took to bed. The first time he did that, I felt my old rage come back. I told the girl, 'What kind of a slut are you to walk into my house to have sex with my husband?' Jaiveer took her in his arms and said, ' She is a distant cousin who stays with me because she is mentally unstable. Don't bother about her.' The woman looked at me with pity in her eyes. And he took her into our bedroom. All night, I sat on the cold kitchen floor, huddled into myself. I rocked myself to sleep. And the next morning, I got the worst beating of my life. Jaiveer pulled out large chunks of my hair and threatened that if I ever spoke up again, he would throw me out of the house.

Looking back today, I often wonder what kind of a man does that to a woman. What can drive someone so insane that they treat someone so badly? Is there no remorse? No feeling? Not a patch of humaneness towards someone else?

And why did I take it? Someone as strong as me? You would think an educated person should have known better. That these things happen only to uneducated women. I still can't find the answers to that. Was it my fear that people would think something was wrong with me? Or the fact that I thought Jaiveer would see reason one day and all would become okay? Or financial dependence? Or did I think it was my karma? My payback time because I had not been a 'good' Indian girl? Or the fear of the humiliation my parents would suffer back home? Or was it the fact that I did not want to admit to myself that I had failed? That smart Simran had made a rotten decision.

Mana is still on the phone. She seems angry. Who would have thought the gentle, unassuming Mana would turn out to be such a stunner. And a hotshot entrepreneur on top of that. She is always busy—organizing this party or the other. I love her stories and gossip about Bollywood and the Mumbai 'Shishi-Puppu' crowd as she calls the air-kissing socialites who dress in the shortest, tightest clothes, and eat nothing! She moves in that social circuit now, but is grounded in her middle-class morality and unfazed with all the glamour. I like that about her.

Mana and I were bosom pals in school. She was my best buddy. The one who complemented me. I was loud, she was quiet. I was naughty, she was straight as a rod. I was always in the limelight, she was the shy, retiring type.

When she got married to KD, I was already in London. Jaiveer took the call and told her that I was off on a project to Africa, and would not be able to make it. He sent a nice gift for their wedding. He would not let me talk to her. He never let me talk to anyone. He was charming on the phone and made my life sound so fancy—I was working late, I was off on a project, I was holidaying at a spa. If only....

One dark, rainy evening in London, Jaiveer had a young girl over. He asked me to get some olives for his lady. There weren't any and his eyes flared up with anger. The young thing simpered and told him to let me go to the supermarket and get some. Jaiveer gave me money, asked me to get olives and be back soon.

I was at the Marks & Spencer checkout counter when I heard a squeal of delight. It was Mana. She was so happy to see me. I cringed. I did not want to meet her. For her to see this fat, ugly Simran. But Mana did not notice. She bounded up to me and hugged me tight. 'My God Simran! It is so good to see you. I have been calling you forever but Jaiveer told me you were traveling. How are you my darling?'

I let myself be hugged and muttered, 'I am good.' Mana went silent. Her pretty face creased up with concern and she said, 'What's wrong Simran?'

I shuffled. I wanted to get away. She held on to my arm. 'Something is wrong Simmo. Tell me.'

It had been so long since someone had said something kind to me. Since someone had shown any concern for me. Since I had been called Simmo. My eyes welled up with tears. I told her, 'Please Mana I need to go. Jaiveer will be waiting for me.'

—I will come home tomorrow Simran. Tell me what time.

—You can't. He'll know.

Mana was puzzled. 'Then meet me somewhere.'

She was persistent and would not relent. So I said, 'Come home at 12. But if you see the Mercedes in the driveway, please drive away.'

She let me go, but was at my door at 12 sharp the next day. I let her in, and I was so ashamed to see her. I could see the questions in her eyes. And her love and concern for me. It was too much for me to handle. My dam broke. I cried and cried, and through my tears told her what had happened to me.

Mana didn't know what to say. She held my hand as I struggled through my story. 'I could never think you would go through all this Simran. You were the smart one. The strong one. You never took nonsense from anyone. Remember the time you took the English teacher Mr. Roy to the principal because he dared to give you a one-armed hug? Or that man you slapped on the bus because he pinched your butt?'

I smiled wanly, 'Yes. I remember. I know Mana. I have thought the same thing. I just waited, because there was nothing else to do. No one to go to.'

I laughed bitterly. 'Will anyone believe these things? I used to wonder in my darkest moments—what made Jaiveer do this? I can understand cheating in a marriage—you do yourself harm. But doing this to me? To his wife? One that he had sworn to protect? What did I do?'

—There has to be a way out. Let me think.

That one week that Mana was in London was the happiest I had been in years. I looked forward to meeting her every day, but I had to take care to not show any behavioral changes in front of Jaiveer.

Mana came up with a plan. She bought a camera and installed it in my room. She hugged me and said, 'Look Simran, it's a horrible thing to even say, but he *is* going to hit you one of these days. Make sure you come in full view of the camera when that happens. And pretend as if you are lurching towards the dresser so you can switch on the recording.'

I tell you. I have never waited to be hit as I waited then. And Jaiveer delivered very well.

It was quite horrible, in part because I egged him on. He beat me up badly and then with a pair of scissors chopped off the only piece of vanity I still retained—my lovely long hair.

That was the very last time he touched me. When he got back home the next evening, fortunately without a woman, Mana was waiting for him.

—I have this recording of you hitting your wife, Jaiveer. And it is not the only copy I have. Even as we speak, my husband has another copy that he will deliver to the police.

Bully a bully and he backs off. Jaiveer was livid, but there was nothing he could do. He glared at me malevolently.

—Now you want to blackmail me you slut?

It feels so good when someone has your back. And they stand up for you. Mana told him, 'Be careful of what you say Jaiveer. Simran will not press any charges. But if you push this, we will report it to the police.'

'What do you want?' he snarled.

—To begin with, her passport. And money in her account. And a written declaration from you that you will leave her alone and not pursue her. If she comes to any harm, and I mean any harm at all, you will have hell to pay.

There is a guardian angel for everyone. For me, it was Mana. She held me together, and managed to get me out of that hellhole. I left that house with Mana that night unable to believe my good luck, and yet petrified that Jaiveer would not let me go this easy.

Jaiveer transferred a million pounds into my account the next day, and I left London. After a nightmarish five years. Forever. Even today, I don't take British Airways flights. I can't get myself to step into London and I still live in fear that Jaiveer may be at Heathrow. It's been 10 years and I still don't have the courage to face him.

I did not go back to India. I went to New York. A friend of mine was at a senior position in P&G and managed to get me a job at Greyhound Advertising. I worked really hard. I was not interested in men and put all my creative energies in getting my work done. Five years later I managed to branch out on my own with two colleagues and we started Firebrand Advertising.

The divorce came through and I never saw Jaiveer again, even though I lived in fear for more than two years. But Jaiveer never attempted to get in touch with me. Finally, I began to unwind and relax. I lost all my extra weight. I started dressing well again. I began to like myself in the mirror. I saw my failures, but the scars of those receded as I began to be successful at work. I started getting male attention again, but I never succumbed—I was not ready for any relationship or heartache. I could not handle a man touching me, and I found it difficult to trust any man again.

New York helped me heal. The buzz of the city gradually began to fill me with the excitement to live again. The changing seasons filled me with hope. I began to appreciate the fact that nothing lasts forever, and that after the harsh winter, there is the beautiful spring that brings everything back to life. Nature destroys and repairs herself every single year and events in life also follow the same cyclical pattern. If there is despair today, tomorrow will bring happiness and hope. I learnt to appreciate my life, and the beauty in it.

Much as I would like to believe that karma has taught Jaiveer a lesson, I have no way of knowing that. It has taken me an incredible amount of time to slowly put back the pieces of my broken spirit together. I don't want to know, because I don't want to open myself to hurt anymore.

Mana came to New York last year. Ever since I moved out of London, we had not managed to meet. We had made plans—to meet in Europe for a holiday, to go to an *ayurvedic ashram* in Kerala, to go to Hawaii—but somehow our schedules had not matched. She had her catering business and kids and I had my fledgling career to take care of.

After nine years, we managed to meet again.

Mana looked good. She had aged—no, that's not an appropriate word, she had grown up well. She glowed. And she still had her lovely infectious smile and laughter. She was so happy to see me. When I took her for a tour of my office, she was like a proud mother hen, clucking at everything, delighted at all I had achieved.

We did not go out that first evening and I insisted she stay with me in my 'bachelorette pad' on Upper East Side. It was a small apartment—just two bedrooms—but it was my haven, my sanctuary. I would come back to it after a day's hard work and unwind. I cooked, I listened to music, I watched TV, I worked on concepts. I was happy there.

Together Mana and I picked up supplies because she insisted on cooking an 'Indian Chinese' meal for me. She knew how much I loved it. We both used to frequent the small vendors near National College in Bandra to eat greasy noodles. I still remember the black wok in which the guy would drop huge amounts of oil, then cabbage and onions and toss it with noodles, soy sauce, vinegar, chilli sauce, and generous amounts of ajinomoto. I am pretty sure my palate would not like that taste today, but it's one of those things you grow up with!

We had fun cooking together, and Mana made awesome chilly chicken and hakka noodles. We sat chatting till late night, and I realized something was amiss. She spoke indulgently of her kids and her mother-in-law, but nothing about her husband. I had never met KD and was curious about him. Back in London I had been too distraught to ask her anything about her life.

So I took the chance then and asked Mana about KD.

And her beautiful eyes welled up with tears as she told me about KD and his philandering. Of the years of suffering that she had endured. 'I am tired of the cycle. It is the same. His sexual liaisons result in lots of attention towards me later. Lots of great sex. More jewelry and exotic holidays. And I console myself saying he can't leave me because of the kids.'

I did not want to be judgmental but I said, 'Really, Mana. I think you need to first be truthful to yourself about why you stay in this marriage. It is not love. It is because of dependency and because this is an easy way out.'

Mana glared at me with bitterness. 'Easy? Is that what it looks like to you, Simran? Living with this constant hurt and anger?'

I held her hand. 'Don't misunderstand me, Mana. You had a choice to make in your marriage. You could have walked out on the marriage and started life afresh.'

—Come on, Simran. You of all people saying that! You know my family.

—Yes I do. So let's say you did not want to shame your family. And therefore decided to stay in the marriage. That's still your choice Mana. And I bet it is not easy to let go of this life now. When he has hit it big. There is a charm in being Mrs. Kapoor. There is a social structure you have created for yourselves and that is difficult to let go of. So somewhere you need to make your peace with all that has happened.

—Simran, you know how difficult it was for you to leave Jaiveer.

—Yes, it was, Mana. For the simple reason that I was trapped in a place where I knew no one, had no access to the phone to call anyone. I could not run because I did not have my passport.

—You could have gone to the police.

I fell silent.

Mana pressed my hand. 'Sorry, I did not mean it like that. You were in a terrible condition, and I don't blame you for what you did not do. My pain is nothing compared to yours.'

You can never tell what happens in people's lives. What trauma those smiles hide and what lies behind that picture-perfect posturing of an ideal family life. I would have never thought Mana's calm facade held such tumult at bay.

'Simran, you can't imagine the shock I went through when I found the names of women in his Blackberry folder; it had my name too. There were dates against each of our names. I remember the dates against mine. Those were the ones when we had made love. It was so horrible. Imagine being in the same folder as his other women. How does he do it? Make love to so many women at the same time?'

'Does he not get the names mixed up?' I asked half-jokingly.

Mana's face fell. 'He called me Deepti once. And when I confronted him later he said he had called me sweetie! I wonder what he would say if he called me Rachna. Or Pooja!'

—He would tell you he was worshipping you! Sorry, I couldn't resist that!

Mana told me of her asthma that became so bad that they had begun keeping an oxygen tank at home. Of the panic attacks that left her breathless. Of sleeping pills she took every time KD was traveling, because she was so bothered with visions of him sleeping with other women. Of working out intensely so that her body would be attractive to KD. Of needing him. Wanting him. Of tears that didn't stop sometimes. Of wanting to protect her children.

All the while that she spoke I thought, *What is it about men, and this stupid dependancy we have on them? We want to get married because we believe that the guy will not leave us. That we will create a happy, loving family with him. Have his babies. Take care of his family. In return, he will respect and love us. And we will be the only woman in our husband's life. What we don't factor in is the fact that as women, we surrender so much in the name of family and its honor, and we are so emotionally and socially tied to the marriage that we fear walking out on it, and the social stigma attached to being a divorced or single woman.*

I looked at Mana and said, 'How do you still live with him, Mana? Would you not find peace if you left him? You are so successful!'

—I can't, Simran. He is a great father.

—So? If he's such a great father, he will support his kids anyway.

—No, Simran. I don't want a broken home for my kids. Not yet. Maybe when they both are grown up and married.

—And what will you be then? You will have lived a life of lies. You will be old. Who will look at you then?

Mana laughed. 'Oh, I am sure I will find a dirty old man for sex!'

'How did you forgive him?' I asked.

Mana said, 'How did you forgive Jaiveer?'

I smiled. 'What was there to forgive? How do you forgive someone who does not think he needs forgiveness? It took me forever to walk with my head held high. To begin to love myself. To stop being afraid of men. I forgave him eventually though. More for the sake of my sanity than his. I had to stop the conversations in my head. I had to stop thinking of what might have been. What had I done for Jaiveer to become a monster? What if I had told my parents? What if I had reported to the police? What if I had poisoned him and killed him?'

Mana said, 'I sometimes shudder to think what would have happened if I had not found you. How long would it have taken for anyone to figure what was happening to you? You know, Simran, you had always responded with so much happiness in your emails.'

I raised my eyebrows, 'Except that I was not writing those emails. I had no access to my emails because Jaiveer had changed my passwords. So he was writing what he thought people would want to hear. That's how my parents never found out.'

—Have you told your parents what had happened?

—No Mana. I did not want them to suffer. I only told them that I could not stay in the marriage. I feel guilty about the fact that I never made it back to India to meet them before they passed away. I could never face them.

I hugged Mana. 'You are my guardian angel, you know, Mana. You came and saved my life. Perhaps that's also what gave me the strength to walk away from the horror. I felt that there is a higher power watching over me. That's the reason I escaped relatively early. Just five years! If that experience means I get a lifetime of happiness and peace, I am grateful for it.'

—Don't you want to get married again?

—Are you kidding me? I don't want a guy, let alone marriage.

—I don't blame you! Let me show you this email I found in KD's phone some months ago.

The email was from some woman called Nivedita. I almost felt sorry for the woman as Mana and I read it out loud.

'Why would you do this to me KD? You knew I was married, and yet, for months you chased me, wooed me, told me I was the love of your life. You told me all the little things about Mana and you, about your children, about your work. You made me feel I was the one. Then why did you change suddenly? Now you refuse to talk to me...tell me that you are busy. You don't respond to my texts, you don't take my calls. You know I can't do anything to you KD—because I am married, and because I cannot risk getting caught at what I did.'

I thought out loud, 'Why do women do it? Get involved with a married man?'

Mana said pensively, 'It is tempting isn't it Simran? If a guy pays you attention when you are much older? You are married to one guy, and he stops appreciating you as anything other than a wife and mother. Your life becomes all about family and kids. And then, someone as charming as KD walks in and starts paying you attention. If I was any of those women I would have been charmed too!

KD can be extremely charming when he wants to be. Look at me. Married to him despite everything—because he knows the right buttons to press.

He knows just what to say, and even now, when I know him so well, and can catch on to his lies, I am amused and amazed at the ease with which he thinks up excuses to slime out of trouble. Maybe that ease is the quality that makes him so successful at work. He can make you feel you are the only truly special person in his life; and the world does not understand the depths of what he feels.'

I mulled over it and said, 'Smart guy your KD. Going for married women. There is no way those poor women will confront him after it is over. They have too much to lose if their husbands find out. And unlike unmarried women, they can't use the threat of an unwanted pregnancy to snag him either!'

Mana smiled sadly, 'Yup. The charmer must also tell them he does not have a fulfilling marriage. That I am not the kind of girl he wanted to marry. That he married me because his parents wanted him to marry me.'

In a deep voice I imitated KD, 'I wish it had been you Nivedita. And that I had met you earlier. We would have been so happy together. You are the kind of woman I always wanted to marry.'

Mana started laughing and got into the act too, 'I would have been a complete person with you. Happy and content. Now, when I get home all I see is that sulky Mana. Her only asset is that she takes good care of my mom and is a good mother. She takes care of me too, but I don't feel emotionally connected to her. And she is so demanding and possessive. She does not even let me keep a female secretary. It is claustrophobic.'

I put on a puppy dog expression, 'I want you so bad that I can't focus on my work. When my friends see me happy these days, they wonder what it is...and I can't tell them it is you who fills my life and my senses.'

—Why don't we leave our spouses? I would leave Mana in a jiffy— only that she is the mother of my kids, and I don't want them hurt.

—But we can be one. We can join together as one.

—And no one does the chicken pose better than me.

I stopped with my mouth half open, the words that had formed there refused to leave my lips. Instead, I said, '*What*?'

Mana explained, 'One of the positions that he is very fond of. He straddles me, and puts my feet on his shoulders. He thinks it helps him enter me (or his girls) deeper. He also thinks it is hugely exciting for me. He pumps and pumps and then withdraws to spill his semen all over me.'

—And I gather you don't enjoy it too much? I asked dryly.

—It's okay. But I would like him closer to my body...to kiss him when he is next to me. Instead, that position reminds me of being harnessed for childbirth—with my soles on his shoulders and my boobs crushed under the weight of my own feet! And the heaving and pushing.

—You are small honey! And so well maintained.

—Thanks Simran. But when you are trying to keep the affection of your husband, you do what you can to make yourself attractive. I know no other way. I got a tummy tuck done as well.

I stopped smiling. 'Why?'

—I don't want to lose him Simran.

—And you think that by going under the knife for the slimeball, he will stay with you?

—Well, I did it in a moment of madness—in one of those phases when he was fucking another woman. And guess what, Simran. He dropped me to the clinic in the morning and came back at night to fetch me. He did not stay next to me. And in the next few weeks, while my body was racked with pain, he did not once touch me, hug me, kiss me, or say a single kind word to me. He was busy wooing the flavor of the month.

I hugged her, 'You poor thing. How you must hurt!'

'I have never shared this with anyone. Sometimes the humiliation kills me, Simran,' Mana's eyes welled up with tears.

—Why don't you make him pay?

—How, Simran? By going out and having an affair? He will throw me out in a heartbeat.

—Let me do it.

Mana was puzzled, 'What do you mean?'

—I mean, I can string him along, and then teach him the lesson of his life.

I got excited with the whole idea.

—I can make him fall for me. And then screw his happiness so much that he will think twice before he tries having an affair again.

—Why would you do it Simran?

—I owe you one Mana. You released me from Jaiveer, and I can release you from KD's womanizing.

—Simran, you don't owe me a thing you mad woman.

I was super excited. I took Mana's hands in mine.

—Do you trust me?

—You are the sister I never had, Simran.

—Then let me do this. KD has never met me. I will make him fall for me. There is only one problem though. I will indulge in cheap love talk with him and possibly sex too. Will you be okay with that?

Mana looked at me in the eye. 'I trust you Simran. And I love that you want to help me. I know you will not fall for him. You love me too much. But there is a bigger problem. After this, I will not be able to call you my friend. You will always be the other woman. I don't want to lose you as a friend.'

I held Mana's hand close to my heart. 'You live in Mumbai and I am in New York. And it is a small price to pay for a lifetime of your happiness. And it will give me closure too. That even if I could never get back at Jaiveer, at least I would have taught some guy a lesson.'

Mana smiled at me. 'Okay. Let's do it. Let's look at it as one more prank that we played on those silly boys in school.'

Oh it was so much fun. Mana and I were both caught up in the excitement of taking KD for a ride. Mana roped Ajit into the plan. He hired my services for the year and asked me to move to Mumbai as a creative director with his advertising firm.

And we watched the fun as it played out. Of KD desiring me and me stringing him along. And then when I had him where I wanted him I started making demands, being hysterical, blackmailing him. I told him to leave Mana and move back to the US with me. When he refused, I hand-delivered photographs of the two of us to his house. I gave them to Mana. She did not open the packet. I also told KD that I would give Mana a video tape of our sexual escapades.

It is incredible how fear can change a man. As long as there was no danger to his marriage and his social position, KD was coolness personified. He could promise me (and the other women) the sun, moon and the stars to get what he wanted. Now, gone was the sexy, suave guy who had tried charming me into his bed. Gone was the big talk about loving only me. Gone was the false bravado about leaving Mana.

Sometimes I think adulterous men are the real sluts. They prostitute their words, and their emotions, for an opportunity to get a woman into bed. There is no thought spared for the havoc they create in their own families or the families of the women they pursue. There is only the itch that must be satisfied at all costs.

But I was relieved to see KD suffer. He did love Mana in his own twisted way and did not want to hurt her or his kids. He was committed to them.

It was not easy for me to carry out the charade either. But all through it, I told myself I was doing it for Mana. For her courage in helping me escape the nightmare that was Jaiveer. For helping me set up my life again.

When KD was exhausted and defeated with me, he finally asked me what I would take to get out of his life. I was sitting in his fancy office. I looked him in the eye and said, 'One million dollars.'

He almost gagged. And then looked at me with disappointment in his eyes, and said, 'So it was all about the money then?'

—Yes. If you won't give me yourself then that is what I will take to get out of your life.

—Don't push it Simran. I can cancel all the accounts with the agency.

—Oh get off the threats KD. My contract with them is over. You can do what you want. It will not impact me.

I could see how he hated me. How he hated himself for having gotten into this relationship with me.

'Don't blackmail me Simran. I did not take advantage of you. This was a two-way street.'

I leaned back into the chair, 'Of course it was. I am not asking you to let me go; you are. I am happy to stay with you. Buy me a house,

and be with me.'
—You know I can't do that.
—Then give me the money.
—You are such a bitch. Not at all what I had thought you were.
I smiled as I stood up, 'Stop behaving like the victim. Transfer the money in my account before this evening. Or, you can go confess to Mana before I send the tapes over. Your wife will love you for that.'
He shook his head in disgust and said, 'Fine. You can have the money and I want you to leave. And never show your slutty face again.'
This time, it did not hurt being called a slut.
KD transferred the money into my account.
Mana walked up to me. I stood up to greet her. And we both hugged. Tight. And then she grinned. 'We did it!'
I gave Mana the one million. That's her money. She took the envelope. Her smile had never looked more beautiful.
I smiled.

Veera

I can't see the sky—or the weather outside. But I do feel it. If I can imagine it, the sky over Mumbai is a dark gloomy one. Big clouds, pregnant with rain loom large over it. Maybe it will be like July 26, 2005. When the clouds burst open and created havoc in the city.

It had been pouring all morning. I was getting ready to go with Piya and Mana to Nariman Point. An Australian expat was moving back to his country and wanted to throw a dinner-to-remember for his friends in India. It was to be a big affair and we had to cater for nearly 300 people. The man wanted to discuss the theme, the decorations, the menu, the return gifts. It was almost like a lavish birthday party. I was not attending the meeting, but I had to pick up the earrings that I had ordered for Namita's birthday. We all planned to meet for lunch after work, and drive home together afterwards.

I never got to Nariman Point. Just as we were about to leave, our man Friday, Pandit, who took care of the business with us, called to say that there was a short circuit at the Khar kitchen. So Piya and Mana went on to the city and I went to Khar.

By 2 p.m., the skies were dark and it seemed like it was seven in the evening. It had been raining since morning, but now rain bore down on us in gray sheets. In that torrential rain, there was no way to try and repair the short circuit, and I had to instruct them to start the back-up generators, because the orders for the evening had to be executed. There was a party at Pali Hill for a hundred guests and another dinner order for 30 people at Juhu.

KD called. He was picking up the children from school because the roads at Bandra-Kurla were filling up with water. He also told Piya and Mana to return home because the forecast was not favorable.

I called Namita. I knew she was at Lower Parel that day, shooting a corporate video for one of those big media companies. I told her to come back home as soon as possible. She said, 'Mom, you always fuss about nothing. I am okay. I will let you know when I leave.' There was nothing you could say to the girl if she had made up her mind.

I went back home to wait for all my children to come back. By three KD was home with my grandchildren. He had managed to get to school on time and get the children before the roads began to fill up. Mana and Piya called at five. They were stuck at the Mahim Causeway. The roads were clogged with traffic, and the water levels looked dangerously high. Many people were abandoning their cars and walking. KD told them to do the same and follow the crowd. He told them to walk behind people and to not venture on their own. He took the car and the driver and drove towards Lilavati, so he could pick them up. It took the girls two hours to walk that one-kilometer stretch, but they got home. Soaking wet but fine.

By six, it was obvious that this was a freak day. The van carrying food to Juhu got stuck in the water-clogged roads. The Pali Hill food was delivered, but they sent a message saying the party had to be canceled.

Then the phone lines collapsed. The mobile phone networks were lost, and there was no way to get in touch with Namita. At around seven in the evening, she managed to get through to Mana's phone and said she was leaving Lower Parel and would be home soon.

The hours passed by, slowly, painfully. At midnight, there was still no sign of Namita. KD did not know where to go look for her. We sat, checking the landline, checking the mobile phones, waiting for her.

At two in the morning, Piya asked me to get some sleep. How could I? I had no idea where my child was or if she was okay.

At four in the morning, the bell rang. And there was Namita. Standing soaked to the bone. Tired, because she had walked all the way from Lower Parel to Bandra.

Hungry. Exhausted.

I breathed then. And my heart felt easy. My child was safe.

Today, I am exhausted with myself. I wonder why I am in this condition. When my body refuses to obey me, and my brain still functions with clarity and my heart still feels, and hurts, and is ready to burst.

I still can't believe that I will never see Namita again. That what KD said is true. That it is the reason Piya has put her head on my chest, and is crying inconsolably.

Namita is dead.

Killed on the Mumbai-Pune Expressway when her team van rammed into an illegally parked truck. I heard Anand tell Piya softly that some bodies are mangled beyond recognition. KD left immediately to get Namita's body back. That boy, Rahul, who Namita used to like in college, is also in the room and is chatting with Mana.

Many years ago, when the children were still small, Gurujitji and I had taken them to Juhu beach in the evening. We walked far away from the hustle bustle of the beach and found a quiet spot beyond the big hotels. I spread out the bedcover I had carried, and Gurujitji went to get *pav bhaji* for all of us to eat. The children were fascinated with the sand and were having a great time making small, uneven structures in it.

Suddenly Namita ran up to me with a shell in her hand. Her curly hair was all unruly, and with a smile that used to melt my heart, she said, 'I got this for you mama.'

I gathered her in my arms and kissed her hair. With her lovely eyes she looked at me and said, 'I know what I want to be when I grow up'. I tugged at her hair playfully and said, 'So soon? You want to grow up so soon?'

She smiled, 'I will be a mama like you when I grow up.'

I could have crushed her with my love for her that day.

A mom like me whose bad karma has come back to haunt her.

A mom like me. Who was scared for her all the time. Scared that someone would know she was Ravi's daughter and Gurujitji would throw me out of the house. That she would be called a bastard.

A mom like me who did not support her photography. She reminded me too much of Ravi. By then I had wanted to remove all traces of him from my life. I did not want Namita to be socially different. I wanted her to get a stable job and get married, and have children and have her own family. I feared for her safety because she was so rash and impulsive.

A mom like me who sent her alone for her abortion. I was horrified and angry and it brought back memories of my own choices. Kal was also an unworthy man. He was a leech. All he wanted was money from KD to invest in his real estate business. When KD told me, I told my son to not entertain him. Any man who married my smart daughter had to be self-made, not looking for favors from her family. And then he walked away with that silly girl Garima.

I could have killed Kal for putting my gentle-hearted daughter through so much pain.

A mom like me who never told her how proud I was of her. That she was the most precious of all my children. She was Ravi. I bore his leaving me, and not looking for me with stoicism, because I had Namita. I poured all my love into my baby girl and lived for her.

I failed my daughter. By not telling her the truth about her birth, by living a life of lies all these years. In my obsession to protect her, I put my daughter through so much pain. Made her feel unwanted and criticized.

In life, you think there will be enough time. Enough time to tell someone you love them. Enough time to visit the countries you've always wanted to visit. Enough time to try the cuisines you want to explore. Enough time to be happy. Enough time to make amends.

There is just never enough time.

I can feel something. I can hear footsteps.

I can feel my eyelids flutter.

I hear the door open.

My eyes open to the artificial light in the room.

It is her. Namita.

And finally, I breathe easy.